The Homeboy

by

Clark E. Hobby

Rev. Dr. Clark E. Hobby

The cover was designed by Charles F. Bofinger, a graduate of Milton Hershey School and a close friend of the author. Pictured is Senior Hall. It overlooks the town of Hershey. Above the school building is a picture of Milton S. Hershey holding one of the original students of Milton Hershey School.

THE HOMEBOY

SIXTH PRINTING 2008
FIFTH PRINTING 2004
FOURTH PRINTING 2003
THIRD PRINTING 2000
SECOND PRINTING 1999

FIRST EDITION

Library of Congress Catalog Card Number: 99-71720

ISBN 0-7880-1444-7

PRINTED IN USA

"Religion that God our Father accepts as pure and faultless is this: to look after **orphans** and widows in their distress and to keep oneself from being polluted by the world." James 1:27

"For I was hungry and you gave me something to eat, I was thirsty and you gave me something to drink, I was a stranger and you invited me in, I needed clothes and you clothed me, I was sick and you looked after me...."

Matthew 25:35-36

ACKNOWLEDGEMENTS

THANKS...

To Milton and Catherine Hershey for the eleven years that I was privileged to be a "Homeboy" in the home/school which they founded.

THANKS...

To my dear wife of forty-nine years, Betty, and for her support as I undertook the work of writing this book.

THANKS...

To Holy Trinity Lutheran Church, a wonderful church family, that I was twice privileged to serve and for their gift of time off to enable me to write my book.

THANKS...

To my grandson, James Hobby, for contributing the art work which heads each chapter.

THANKS...

To my Milton Hershey School brother, Charles Bofinger, whose art work graces the walls of my study and who graciously consented to do the cover of this book.

THANKS...

To a host of people who encouraged me to do the writing and who were helpful in reading the material and who were helpful with suggestions during the course of my writing. To Dick Lewis a MHS graduate whose technical skill regarding printing helped immensely . To Betsy Ahlersmeyer, a teacher of journalism, and Lynda Eade, an English teacher, who read the manuscript and offered constructive criticism.

THANKS...

To a dear friend, Dr. Joseph Brechbill, who helped make my work a bit easier with his suggestions and overall resourcefulness.

THANKS...

To all of my HIS brothers who were ahead of me and who provided me with great role models.

To all of my HIS brothers who were part of the distinguished class of '47 and with whom I shared experiences that will never be forgotten.

To all administrators, teachers, houseparents, and staff personnel who helped shape what I value most in life and who went beyond the call of duty because they genuinely cared about Homeboys.

To all of my Milton Hershey School brothers and sisters — past, present, and future — who though once the victims of adversity share with me the joy and blessing of being one of "Milton's kids."

THANKS...

To Almighty God for His infinite and redeeming love and for His providence at work through the unending philanthropy of Milton Snavely Hershey

**"HIS DEEDS ARE HIS MONUMENT
HIS LIFE OUR INSPIRATION"**

FOREWORD

It was an emotional moment for me. I returned to the place that I call home; it is referred to as, "the sweetest place on earth."

I had taken my church's youth group on a visit to Hershey, Pennsylvania, which I've done every three years for the past twenty-six years. After spending three and a half days in "Chocolate Town, U.S.A.," the group was reluctantly preparing for departure. The plan was for us to stay overnight in Pittsburgh, so we were facing a trip of three and a half hours on the road. Arrangements for that evening included a banquet and lots of fun in a motel with an indoor swimming pool. Even with all of that ahead for us, the thrilling experiences which we shared in Hershey caused us to linger awhile.

Before turning the loaded vehicles westward, I took my group of high school boys and girls to Hershey Cemetery; it was one of the sites that we had not yet visited. The cemetery sits high, overlooking the town. In the center of the cemetery there is a large, impressive monument where the remains of Milton S. Hershey and his lovely wife, Catherine, are buried.

Teenagers visiting a cemetery and finding it of interest is not an everyday occurrence, but the decision to take them there proved to be a prudent one! At the close of that day, they talked about their visit to the cemetery as definitely being one of the highlights of their Hershey excursion.

The kids were thrilled when we drove down Chocolate Avenue and they saw for the first time the street lights in the shape of Hershey kisses (every other one unwrapped baring its chocolateness); they were in awe when we drove up the lane toward Founders Hall — a breathtaking view. They were like little children when disembarking from the ride at Chocolate World, anticipating the free candy which is generously given to visitors. They talked a mile a minute as they hurried through the gates into Tudor Square, Hersheypark's entrance, but who would have thought that these young people would in unison respond with reverence, as they quietly stood with me by the graves of those very special people whose philanthropy opened the door to opportunity for thousands and thousands of disadvantaged children. There is no honor in being an orphan, but there is great honor in being one of Milton's boys.

The cemetery visit enabled me to fulfill a personal commitment. I make the cemetery my last stop after each visit to Hershey. In addition to the graves of the Hersheys, I kneel for prayer at the graves of buddies, Bob and Jim, who grew up with me in "The Home". They were more than just close friends; they were my Hershey brothers. Together we had shared happy times and times of struggle and all that the teen years bring with them. Growing up in this context, we developed an enduring bond. Jim died within a decade of my graduation (he was a year younger than I); Bob passed through the valley of the shadow of death many years later. I have been left with cherished memories of experiences in which they shared and which neither death nor time can erase.

People often ask me, "What was it like to grow up in an orphanage?" At Hershey we were orphans, but we never referred to the Hershey Industrial School as an orphanage; for us it was "The Home", and we were Homeboys and very proud of it!

Why and how did I get to this genuinely unique home/school? What did I experience through those early eleven years of my life? This is my story! As I put it on paper, it aroused in me anger, laughter and tears; it facilitated my telling — for the first time — some experiences that previously were extremely difficult to share. For me, the telling of this story has been a cathartic experience.

Founders Hall Statue

THE HOMEBOY

I.
PROLOGUE

In 1909 Milton and Catherine Hershey (she died in 1915) founded a home/school for orphan boys. Milton, the "Chocolate King", hoped that he would live to see one hundred boys enrolled in "The Home." By the time of his death in October of 1945, there were one thousand boys who comprised the student body. Today, fifty-three years after his death, there are well over a thousand boys and girls enrolled.

When I was a student at "The Home", boys in the fifth grade and under lived in what we referred to as the cottages. They were housing units that were clustered together and within walking distance of the Fanny B. Hershey Memorial School. The summer prior to entering sixth grade, students were sent from the cottages to farm homes. On the farms boys ranging from sixth grade up to and including the senior year of high school lived as families with two sets of houseparents. There were twenty to twenty-one boys on each of the farms; it was in this context that the boys learned to get along with one another, and they were taught to do basic farm chores. Mr. Hershey believed that an idle mind was the devil's work shop.

Yes, we learned to work, and we were taught to assume responsibility. When one violated "the rules", demerits were handed out to the violator. This meant that privileges were reduced ; one soon learned that it didn't pay to buck the system. Extra hours of work, no visit to town to attend a movie or Hersheypark, and sitting on the porch while the other boys played were just some of the ways demerits were erased. The duration of being without privileges was commensurate with the number of demerits that one had.

On occasion a boy was transferred from one student home to another. How did the transfer take place? I recall moving from the cottage, Kinderhaus, to farm home Arcadia. With my clothing I "hitched" a ride on the meal truck which was taking food prepared at the central kitchen to the various farms, one of them being Arcadia. It wasn't a fancy way to move, but it got the job done.

It was assumed that when a student was admitted to "The Home", it would be his home until graduation from high school. Today there are over seven thousand who are alumni, and there are many hundreds more who once were homeboys but who for one reason or another left "The Home" prior to graduation.

People everywhere know about Hershey candy, but what is not so well known is the philanthropy of a great and generous man who dedicated his entire fortune to helping needy, disadvantaged kids. Recently the United States Government honored Milton Snavely Hershey with the issuance of a postage stamp; this was not done because Mr. Hershey was a great industrialist, but because he was a great philanthropist, a twentieth century humanitarian.

It is my hope that by writing this book, someone who reads it will facilitate a needy child in becoming one of "Milton's kids".

II.
ON MARKET STREET

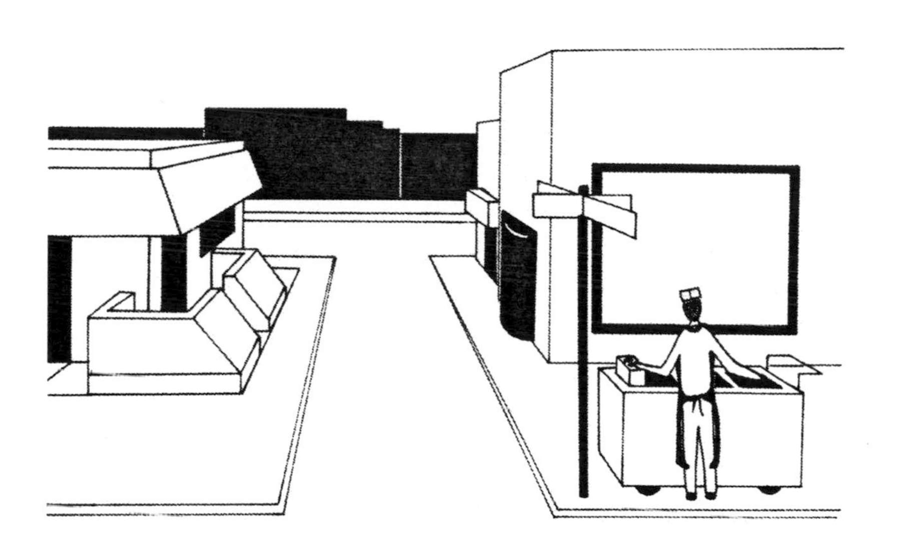

The steel mill town of McKeesport, Pennsylvania, was a busy place in 1917. The First World War was being fought, and our nation was in the midst of it.

Not only was steel needed to keep production of arms at its highest level, but the country's young men were needed for the battle field.

In 1917 and in McKeesport, a young woman by the name of Frances Hopton was taking time away from the convent; she needed to make an important decision — a decision that would greatly affect the rest of her life. She needed to prayerfully seek the guidance of God. Would she stay in the convent and go on to Holy Orders, as a nun? It was a big decision for a young woman to make.

In the same city and the same year, a young man by the name of Andrew Hobby was home on leave, prior to being sent to the front in Europe. He enlisted at an early age, having persuaded his parents to sign the necessary papers.

The young woman on leave from the convent and the young man on leave from the Army had a chance encounter. For them it was love at first sight. Apparently they had a lot of things in common. Both Andrew and Frances possessed a zest for life, and they had the ability to maintain their sense of humor even when facing tough times.

There was, however, one big obstacle which they had to overcome: it had to do with religion. She was from a Roman Catholic family, and he was from a

Frances M. Hobby
(Mother)

Andrew J. Hobby, Sr.
(Father)

Albert & Clark shortly before their mother's death.

Grandparents Hobby

strong Protestant background. They lived and met in an era that was not especially friendly to what was often referred to as a "mixed marriage." Their respective families looked with suspicion on mixing a Roman Catholic and a Protestant.

Andrew and Frances were determined to marry and for a good reason: they were in love! Though they didn't get to enjoy many years together, they had a good marriage.

One of the vexing problems that plagued them throughout the years of their relatively short marriage was totally unrelated to religion; it was a problem of debilitating health.

Andrew entered the military at age seventeen, and he was sent overseas to serve as an infantryman in France. In a battle which took place in the Argonne Forest (France), he became the victim of chemical warfare. He lived valiantly with the horrific effects of mustard gas, which seventeen years later took his life. Those years were at best difficult and painful.

In the last years of his life, he and Frances, with their rapidly expanding family, lived in what one could call a "condo," but in reality, it was a very modest apartment above a tire store on Market Street.

Caught in the grip of the Great Depression, caring for her ailing husband, expecting her eighth child and looking after her seven children consumed all of the energy Frances could muster. From all reports, she was not one to complain; she made the best of each new day, a believer that God would grant grace sufficient for every need.

One day, her worst fear became reality. Her beloved husband, with his incredible sense of humor, was gone. What was she to do? What could she do? Unfortunately, she was left without financial assistance. The Social Security Act was just coming into existence, and at the time, it was without all of the umbrella programs which we today normally associate with it.

Andrew, a veteran, who suffered from chemical warfare, should have been the recipient of the Purple Heart. It is also sad, but true, that the government was extremely slow in providing assistance to him and later to his widow. Frances had died before any assistance arrived.

Two months after her father's death, Audrey, the baby, was born. This brought to eight the number of children in the family. Within a year of her husband's death, Frances was taken to the hospital diagnosed with pneumonia. Without the will to live and without benefit of the so-called miracle drugs, she passed from this earthly life. (Some said that she died of a broken heart, unable to recover from the loss of her beloved husband.) Up to the day of her death, the family lived in the upstairs apartment on Market Street.

Left behind were eight orphaned children in the midst of an economic depression. The paternal grandparents took control of the situation. They knew

The eight Hobby children as adults.
Front: Audrey, Minerva, Betty, and Eva. Back: Albert, Jack, Clark, and Andrew, Jr.

that whatever they could do would of necessity be on a temporary basis. Grandfather Hobby was a retired policeman; he and grandmother were living on a meager pension.

Breaking up is hard to do, but that is precisely what had to be done! The family would never be together again to celebrate a Christmas, Easter, or birthdays. We were orphans, and life was going to be very, very different for us.

An aunt and uncle adopted the baby (Audrey). From the time that she was taken out of the Market Street apartment, we were not permitted to refer to her as our sister; we were told that she now had a new family.

Albert, the next to the youngest, went to live with an aunt who was a widow. She took him on a temporary basis. The eldest of the girls, Eva, also went to live with this aunt.

Jack, Minerva, Betty, Andrew, Jr. and I went to live with our grandparents on Packer Street. They had a modest home with limited space, but they were willing to do what they could until something of a more permanent arrangement could be worked out.

How my grandfather learned about the Hershey Industrial School (now known as the Milton Hershey School) located at Hershey, Pennsylvania, remains a mystery to me. It can best and only be described as the wonderful providence of God.

Berta Harm, a psychologist, was sent from the Hershey School to our Packer Street residence to administer a series of tests.

One of the requirements for admission to the school was quite clear: one had to be of average or above average intelligence. Family members told me that they were amazed at one of my responses to a question that was asked of me: "Clark, why do people have eye lashes?"

I responded: "To keep dirt out of their eyes." Not a bad response for a child who had just reached his seventh birthday!

Of the four boys, I was the only one being considered for Hershey. Why didn't Andy go with me? That is a question for which I have no answer. Rather quickly, word was received that there was a place for me at Hershey. The need was obvious and I apparently satisfied all of the admission requirements. The elderly grandparents must have felt a sense of relief upon being informed that I had a home to which I could go.

Minerva, Betty, and Andrew, Jr. were already enrolled at Scotland Orphanage located near Chambersburg, Pennsylvania. It was a military school and operated by the state and veterans' organizations. Since our father was a veteran, my sisters and brother had absolutely no problem gaining admittance. As you can see, little by little, the Andrew Hobby family was being dispersed.

At this point in time, Albert was only five years of age, and the family made a decision to keep him at home until he reached the age of seven. As a seven year old, he would eventually join me at Hershey.

Eva, the eldest of the girls, stayed with an aunt until finishing high school. Often she would stay over on Packer Street with our elderly grandparents. She took on the role of surrogate mother for Albert and me — she was the one who wrote to us and remembered us with cards on our birthdays and other holidays. Also, the few occasions that we were back in McKeesport for two-week vacations (I had five in the eleven years that I was enrolled at Hershey), she was the one to coordinate our activities when we vacationed, visiting relatives, etc.

Brother Jack, the eldest of the eight children, stayed only a short time with our grandparents; this could have been predicted because he was a "spirited" young man. While he was too far advanced in age to qualify for an orphanage, he did learn about and went into the Civilian Conservation Corp, a governmental program designed to put young men into useful service during a time when jobs were really scarce. This was also a way of getting youth off the streets and into some sort of disciplined life.

While in the CCC Camp, Jack excelled as a boxer, and I have often wondered if this was a means by which he could vent his anger over losing his parents and family.

The years on Market Street were our last years together as a family. The final year on Market Street was a nightmare: father died after suffering seventeen years the ravages of chemical warfare, and within a year of his death, our mother died.

III.
ON THE TOP STEP

The time had come for me to leave McKeesport, the place where I was born and a city to which I would never return as a resident.

"Clark," my grandmother said to me, "it is time for you to go to bed. You will need a good night's sleep because you have a long, tiring trip ahead of you tomorrow."

Reluctantly, tearfully, I trudged up the stairs to the bedroom which Andy and I had shared. I didn't know — how could I know — what was ahead for me? Unable to sleep, I was lying in bed thinking about the changes that had taken place in my life. It was scary. I tossed and turned in my bed. Andy, with whom I shared the bed and on whom I relied, wasn't there so I couldn't talk things over with him; and Albert had been living up on Jenny Lind Street with Aunt Eva, but had he been there, he was too young to give me advice or encouragement.

Sister Eva, who was old enough to comfort and advise, wasn't with me that night either. Was it planned this way? Did my family think it would be easier for me if there wasn't a long night of trying to make the separation? That remains an unanswered question. I only remember that it was dark, and I was lonely and scared.

After a little time had passed and I had brushed all the tears away, there was a knock at the door. After the door shut (a little slam to have it latch properly), I could hear muffled voices. I listened intently. They sounded like familiar voices; quickly, I jumped

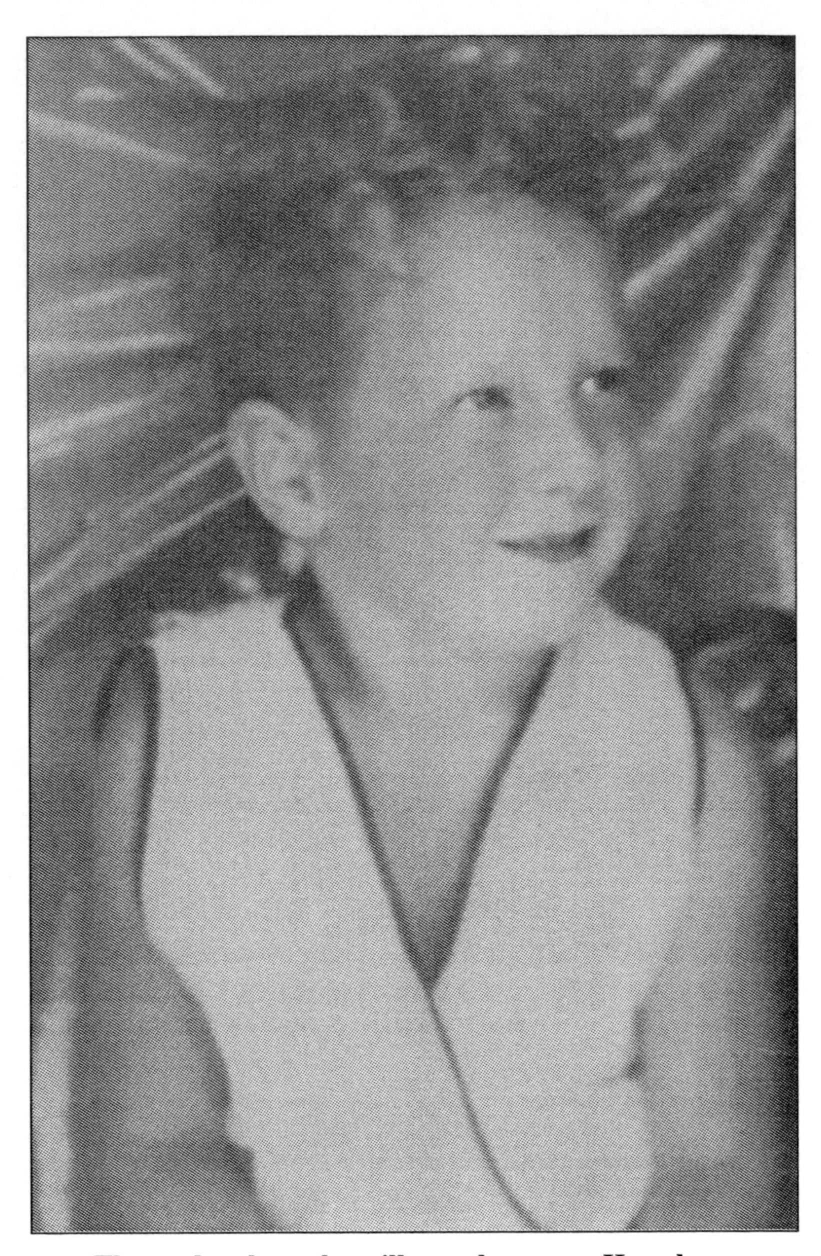

The orphan boy who will soon become a Homeboy.

out of bed and headed for the top step which made listening easier. The steps from the upstairs emptied into the dining room off of which was the living room.

There I perched on the top step! The voices were clearer, and immediately I recognized them. A family from my grandparents' church had come, and I quickly discovered the reason for their coming: they were pleading with my grandparents to let them adopt me.

From the top step, it became crystal clear that someone wanted to make a home for me. This family had befriended me at church. They occupied the pew in front of my grandparents, and initially they would pause to chat with us. Then they began taking me home with them after the church service; they owned a chicken farm out on the Dixie Highway.

As time passed, they not only took me to spend Sunday afternoons with them, but when summer rolled around, they kept me for a week at a time. They were good people who were parents of three daughters. It was their desire to have a son, and since they didn't (couldn't?) it was easy for them to become very fond of a little orphan boy. They even encouraged me to call them Daddy and Mommy, which I did.

Obviously, at some point, this family conceived the idea of adopting me. They knew that my grandparents were too advanced in years to assume the responsibility of raising me and my other siblings.

By the time that I was preparing to leave for "The Home" at Hershey, I was seven years of age.

There they were on the eve of my departure for Hershey, and they had come to my grandparents' home not to say goodbye but to seek adoption privileges. Their mission was to convince my grandparents that they were able to provide me with a good home. After all, the baby had been adopted, why not me?

From the top step, I listened in on their conversation. There was one question which definitely influenced my grandparents' decision, and it was this: "Will you change the boy's name?" "Yes," they replied. My grandfather then responded, "Our answer is no!" From the top step, I heard the reason that my grandparents would not consent to my being adopted. Grandfather said, "He was born a Hobby and he will die a Hobby." The family name was too important to sacrifice. While I couldn't understand then, I do now. Mr. and Mrs. P. had gotten their answer. After a few more minutes of conversation, the visit ended and I heard the front door close. They were gone. My fate had been sealed!

IV.
ON MY OWN

At the crack of dawn, after hugs, kisses, and tears, my grandmother Hobby urged me to be brave, promised me her prayers and never looked back when she headed for the house. I kept looking, hoping she would return to the car and say, "It's all off. I won't let them take you away." But she didn't come back; it must have been too painful for her to even watch us drive away.

Uncle Bill was the driver, grandfather was in the passenger's seat, and I was in the backseat. It was a bleak morning...still dark, as we slowly headed down the Packer Street hill.

I thought to myself, "Well, grandfather was right. He told me that I would be on my own." It was a long, tiring day. Two hundred miles in 1936 was a long trip. The Pennsylvania turnpike had not yet opened. We had to climb some pretty steep mountains with trucks inching their way ahead of us. To pass was risky business. One had to be patient; it was time-consuming.

On a few occasions, grandfather or Uncle Bill would invite my participation in a discussion that ensued, but in those days, kids were to be seen and not heard. So I had to pretty much entertain myself. Now and then, one of the adults in front would point out a deer or some other form of wildlife. It seemed to infuse a little excitement at least for a few minutes; it gave us something to talk about.

It was early afternoon when we arrived in Hershey. The admittance process was immediately begun; everyone was kind to us. It seemed like there was a lot that we had to do. Finally, I was told, "Clark, your new home will be Evergreen. You will be very happy there with all the other boys." Evergreen was one of the homes which housed twenty to twenty-five boys who were in fifth grade and under.

When we arrived at Evergreen, the housemothers were introduced to us; we spent a little time together in what they called "the visitor's room." Soon the housemother in charge announced that supper was ready and that there was a place at the table for me. "Thank you," I said, "but I am not hungry."

Grandfather said with emphasis, "Run along, Clark. You will enjoy meeting the other boys. We will see you when you are finished with supper." He was not one with whom you'd negotiate. When he told you to do something, you did it. (Keep in mind that he had been a policeman, and he expected compliance from us.) Obediently, I went with the housemother to the place that was set for and assigned to me. As soon as the boys were dismissed from the table (I was told that you don't leave until all are dismissed), I made a beeline for the visitors' room. To my dismay, it was empty! Grandfather and Uncle Bill were gone! They had tricked me. While I didn't know it then, it was going to be two years before I would see a relative again.

How could they do this to me, I wondered? I felt deceived, betrayed, and abandoned. I felt like I was on my own, and I was frightened. As I think back to that day, I try to place myself in my grandfather's situation. What did he feel? Did he sleep that night, or conversely could he sleep better that night knowing another one of Andrew's boys was in "good hands"?

For a child of seven to be stripped of family and torn from the world with which he was familiar had to be traumatic; within a year, I had lost both of my parents and now I was losing my family. I cannot remember back any further than the night prior to my leaving for Hershey, and those details are vivid...it's like life began for me when I stepped out of the car onto the ground in Hershey.

I had walked into a new world, surrounded by all new faces — adults and children — and I knew that I was on my own. It was a profoundly emotional and psychological experience for me. During my first six years at Hershey, I lived in five different homes. The student homes were referred to as "units."

So...new boys, new houseparents, and new surroundings were a seemingly never-ending part of my life. The one thing that was constant in my early life was change! From the time that I was five and up to the time of my thirteenth birthday, I experienced seven sets of adults to whom I was answerable; it began with my parents, then grandparents, after whom came a series of five sets of houseparents. God has gifted even small children with the amazing capacity to adjust to circumstances which at the time may, indeed, be horrific.

Fanny B. Memorial Building Elementary School.

CHRISTMAS DAY AT THE HOMESTEAD.

The Homestead birthplace of Milton S. Hershey
Drawing by Charles Bofinger

It didn't take long until "The Home", in every sense of the word, became home for me. The other boys with whom I lived, studied, and played became my family. The bonding of Homeboys is incredible. This is evidenced in the fact that there is a fierce loyalty among the alumni. Maybe that is a by-product of one having to be "on his own."

Evergreen was one of a number of cottages, all in a row; they were within walking distance of the Fanny B. Hershey Memorial Elementary School (named after Milton's mother). Entrance into the second grade was my introduction to "The Home." Friendships were established, with some of them lasting a lifetime.

The Class of '47 was already beginning to form. Some who were part of it in those early years dropped out, while others at various grade levels were admitted along the way.

Our elementary school was really quite nice. It housed not only classrooms, but also such facilities as a swimming pool, auditorium, barber shop, medical center, etc. It was part of a complex which included The Homestead, the birthplace of Milton Hershey, the central kitchen (meals were centrally prepared for all the student homes and trucked out to them), the supply room and the clothing room. All of these resource centers were collectively referred to as "The Main."

In early summer of 1937, a few third graders at Evergreen (I was one of them) were sent with other third graders, from various cottages, to the student home, Harpers. How and why we were selected is another mystery. It had nothing to do with our progress, or lack of it, in the classroom. Personally, I am convinced that selection was based on how well, or not so well, a boy was adjusting to life in "The Home."

The concept at Harpers was one of cohesiveness. The third graders who were chosen were for the most part isolated from not only the other third grade students but from the entire student body. The only time that Harper boys interacted with other Homeboys was at chapel on Sunday morning. As soon as the worship service was over, the Harper boys were immediately bused back to their student home miles from town.

We had our own one-room school and Monday through Friday, Miss Snavely came to teach us. The group of which I was a member (1937-38) was the last to reside at Harpers. We had two sets of houseparents: one was in charge and the other was in an assisting role.

After living together for one year with no opportunity for outside friendships, we grew very close to one another, learning to depend upon each other.

Our one-room school was originally the carriage house for the mansion, which was now a student home. The large house and school sat on a number of acres. The back acreage, which was pretty much in its natural state, provided us with an opportunity to explore and for those interested, an opportunity to fish. It was there that I had my first encounter with a snake; it was one of the braver boys who actually killed the snake, but the event gave us eight-year-olds something to talk about and to attach to our collection of memories.

One of my favorite periods in the day at Harpers was reading time. Miss Snavely instructed us to put all books and papers into our desks to eliminate any distractions. She would read stories to us. During the course of the year, we listened to her read such books as Oliver Twist and Heidi. I sat on the edge of my seat and listened intently to every word that Miss Snavely read.

I was "on my own" and reading time may have offered me an opportunity to escape reality. Family members and friends have often referred to me as a survivor; to whatever degree that is true, I attribute it to those early years when I was literally "on my own." Is it any wonder that Heidi (who called out for her grandfather) captured my interest?

At Harpers — it was late fall or winter — one of the boys fell and injured his knee which developed into cancer and which very quickly took his life. We, his classmates, were confronted with the reality of death once more! There were no counselors rushed in to assist us in dealing with this loss. We turned to each other and leaned on one another in that time of crisis.

Student Home Harpers for 3rd graders.

That very winter of 1938, I became quite ill. Our student homes had the bedrooms upstairs, and at Harpers, that upstairs was way up. Now and then, the housefather (probably more than I realized) would check on me. Through the day my temperature was rising, and by supper time I was delirious. Under the cover of darkness, the housefather drove me to the Hershey hospital; I was wrapped in blankets, laid on the seat of the Harpers' bus, and off we went into the night. At the hospital, I was diagnosed as having the German measles.

This was my first recollection of being told about the danger of biting down on a thermometer while having my temperature taken. Also, I gained great respect for the nurse who was assigned to care for me. I can still see her in that magnificently white, starched dress with cuff links. She was genuinely caring and, in every respect, truly impressive!

Because I had something highly contagious (one of my buddies from Harpers with the same malady soon joined me at the hospital), I was placed in isolation. It was either the nurse or the houseparents who brought me marbles, and I was told that before I left, the marbles must be sterilized. Frankly, life in the hospital was so good that my return to health was a bit disappointing. Think about it! My meals were brought to my bed, I took a nap each afternoon, and after waking up, I was given a large glass of chocolate milk. When my buddy, Paul, joined me, it only got better. But one day, I was well enough to return to Harpers.

3rd graders — last group to live at Harpers (Clark at the right end of row 1.)

Easter that year brought me a big surprise. The mother of one of the boys gifted me with a large decorated, chocolate Easter Egg; this gift and the giver would never be forgotten. That year, I received an Easter card from Grandma and Grandpa Hobby and Aunt Eva, making that Easter very special and memorable.

The only negative experience that I had at Harpers was related to "nail check." Without any warning, the housefather inspected our fingernails. If there was evidence of nail chewing, offenders were spanked. I was always an offender, so my thought was, "Forget the inspection, I'm ready to take my punishment."

Before we left Harpers, the summer of 1938, I had my first visitors. It had been two years since I was "on my own" and had seen a member of my family. They had come not specifically to visit with me, but their mission was to bring my younger brother, Albert, for admission. Unfortunately, they came to see me after he was admitted, which meant that he was not with them, and I desperately wanted to see him. I'd have to wait until Sunday at chapel before seeing my younger sibling whom I greatly missed.

There were so many questions that I had for my family members; however, their time was limited, and before I realized it, they were gone. Albert was assigned to cottage "F" (Fosterleigh) just north of Evergreen, my first student home.

After the school year ended, we left Harpers. It was closed as a student home and later sold (today it is a bed and breakfast). Once more, we were sent to different student homes; this time, I was sent to Kinderhaus. It was used to house fourth and fifth graders. I was "on my own," so it didn't really matter where I was sent. Kinderhaus was one of the first homes used to house the boys — the first being The Homestead (Milton Hershey's birthplace).

I was happy at Kinderhaus. I liked its location, and I liked the people who were in charge. We could not have had better supervision. When we sat on the front porch, we were able to observe the traffic on Governor Road; also, the trolley car ran past our house on its way to Campbelltown. On those rare occasions when we went into town (Hersheypark, etc.), we would board the trolley across the street in front of our student home, so there was a lot going for us.

At Kinderhaus it was a common sight to see the mounted State Police in single file making their way down Governor Road. The commander on a large white stallion led the procession; it was an impressive sight, especially for fourth and fifth graders.

One summer day, when we were playing baseball in the field west of Kinderhaus, we got the surprise of our lives: Milton Hershey's automobile pulled alongside Governor Road and parked; his chauffeur opened the rear door so that Milton could get a better view of "his boys" at play. Seeing him, we waved to him. Protocol would not have permitted us to go running up to his car, as the school's movie depicts; to have done that would have been viewed as inappropriate. Even fourth and fifth graders who had spent a few years in "The Home" would have known not to do that.

In the summer between my fourth and fifth grades, I was summoned to the hospital. Before leaving Kinderhaus and walking the quarter of a mile to the hospital, the housemother informed me that I was to have my tonsils removed. It was not unusual for a boy who had chronic colds, sore throats, etc. to undergo a tonsillectomy (something common in many households and not just unique to the Hershey Industrial School). Slowly I walked along Governor Road; I was in no hurry to arrive. I was "on my own." It was a nice walk from Kinderhaus and would have been more enjoyable under more favorable circumstances.

Admittance procedures were followed. This time I was assigned to a bed in a ward with other boys whom I knew. The next morning, each of us having tonsils removed was given a blanket, and we took a seat in the solarium. One by one, our names were called; at the appropriate time, a hospital employee would meet and take us to the elevator for a ride to the second floor. It was on the second floor that we were prepared for surgery and then had to wait to be wheeled into the operating room. Can you picture a group of fourth and fifth graders sitting, waiting for

Student Home Kinderhaus (4th & 5th graders).

surgery, pretending that "it's no big deal"? To be honest about it, I was picturing in my mind various escape routes, but I knew that in the end, I would have to submit. A cleaning lady who, sensing our anxiety, said, "Boys, you have to be strong! Everything will be okay." Being on her end of the mop handle, that was easy advice to give. But she was a compassionate lady, and it was her way of trying to console us.

The two years at Kinderhaus were enjoyable years. The housemother in charge was a godly woman; she was genuinely dedicated to the task of caring for the boys in her charge. She could be firm, but she was always fair. We knew the rules and breaking them had consequences.

There were evenings when we were ready for bed, and Miss Barker would announce to us that we were going to be given a treat; she would invite us into her apartment, where we would sit on the floor in front of her radio and listen to one of our favorite radio programs — the most popular being "The Shadow". Wisely, this treat was rare, so that we didn't take it for granted. Another not-too-often treat came after we were nestled in our beds. The lights were out, and we were not supposed to talk, so it was dark and quiet; out of the silence came this soft voice saying, "Open your mouth." Into each little mouth, she would drop a piece of candy. We were not given a lot of candy, as one might suppose, so this little treat was greatly appreciated. These various treats were symbols of the love that Miss Barker had for the boys for whom she was responsible. She, like a host of others, did her job well.

At "The Main," the smaller children were expected to do chores commensurate with their ability to perform them. The School had a large truck patch where many of the vegetables were raised and then canned for future consumption. During the canning season the boys who lived in the cottages would carry the cans from the place of canning to the storage area. Early on, we were taught responsibility and had instilled in us the work ethic.

After my fourth grade year, Aunt Eva came from the Pittsburgh area to take both Albert and me on a two weeks' vacation. I was in "The Home" for three years before returning to my hometown. Albert had just finished his first year in "The Home", so he was more fortunate in this regard. Each boy was permitted an annual two weeks' vacation; however, some of us didn't have family who could afford costs related to the vacation's transportation, etc.

While Albert and I did enjoy a vacation in the summer of 1939, that same opportunity was not available to us the following year. Sensitive to the situation, the school administrators sent my brother and me on a vacation to one of the farms. For the entire two weeks, we were guests and not expected to perform chores of any kind. We watched the older boys as they milked cows. They told us that chocolate milk came from the cows who were fed Hershey bars; we watched them make hay and were on the sidelines as they hoed corn. We also enjoyed watching that farm home play rival farm homes in baseball.

Athletics were an important part of our lives. In the elementary grades ("The Main"), we were taught gymnastics such as swinging on the rings. We were taught the rudiments of wrestling and boxing. We also learned how to swim, to play basketball, baseball, and soccer (the latter was a game in which many of the boys could participate, at the same time).

In gym class at "The Main," our physical education instructor was popular with the boys. However, he had a finger missing and anytime that one of us got out of line, we were "thumped" on the head with the teacher's stump. Quickly, we got the message! When he spoke, we listened.

The one thing that every boy soon learned regardless of his entry level is that you don't snitch on another boy. This was one thing that was not tolerated. The houseparents didn't encourage it, and the other boys emphatically deplored it. It was not an acceptable practice.

The boy who was "on his own" was finishing fifth grade with an eye to the farm. Every boy at "The Main" knew that life would be vastly different out on the farm, but each of us was well aware of the fact that going to the farm was something for which he had been preparing. No one wants to be a "little guy" forever. While it was scary thinking about moving again and to something totally new, we were "Homeboys" and we were up to the task!

V.
ON THE FARM

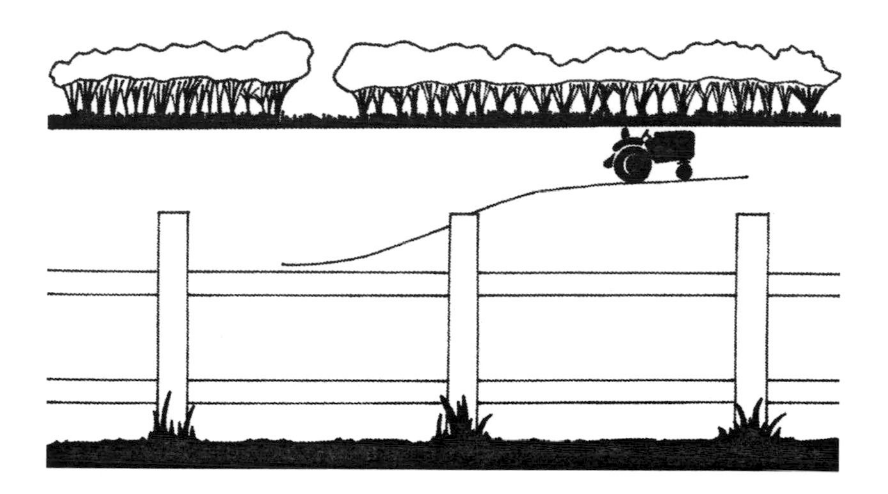

In early summer of 1940, I was transferred to the farm and a number of changes were about to occur. In the fall, I would be heading to "The Hill" for school. Soon I would be turning in my knickers and be fitted for long trousers, and on the farm, I was going to be expected to do regular chores. This meant that there would be less playing and more working. While it was exciting to move to the farm, it was also scary because, up to this point, most of my housebrothers were within a year or two of my age. At each of the farms, the boys ranged from the sixth grade to seniors in high school. The age gap was much wider. There were eighteen boys on the farm to which I was transferred (including me). Two other sixth graders and I arrived at Farm Home Arcadia in late summer. We were referred to as "The New Guys." One of the other two, Dick, had been with me at Harpers, so for us, it was a reunion, and we became roommates. This helped because at night we could lie in bed and discuss what was going on in our lives.

Dick and I would be separated a year and a half later when Arcadia was closed as a farm home. However, the bond between us that began at Harpers and strengthened at Arcadia was so strong that following graduation, with two other classmates, we enlisted in the Air Force. We were part of a family, and the family's name was The Hershey Industrial School.

At "The Home," moving from the cottages to the farm was really a big deal! I can't speak for the practices at other farms, but at Arcadia, the new guys were initiated. After Arcadia, I was transferred to Willow Wood, and at that student home, initiation was not practiced.

We had one boy who was at the center of the initiation and probably was the one who instigated it. Out of such a large number of boys, it is not surprising that one would emerge a "bully." However, at the cottage level, a Homeboy learned that snitching was not the way situations should be resolved. "Squealers" were not looked upon with favor. Generally when bullying got out of hand, an older boy would restrain things and put an end to a bully's activity. Conflicts were usually handled by the boys without knowledge or involvement of a houseparent. There were exceptions, of course, but the older guys would generally look out for the younger ones, "calling off" those who tended to harass. I can't remember a conversation with any of my peers on this subject, which leads me to believe that little of this activity went on. The only other farm on which I lived and where I spent five and a half years had none of it.

By the time we reached the farm, if we didn't already have a nickname, it didn't take long for one to be assigned. At Arcadia, in those early months, some of my house brothers thought that I was a "sweet guy." Even then, I was sensitive to the feelings of others; I'd rather have my feelings hurt than to hurt someone else. So...what is it that is sweet and used in Hershey candy? Sugar! From that time forth, I was referred to as "Shug."

Arcadia (#20) was located a long distance from town. Perhaps, it was the student home farthest from the center of activity, and for this reason, during the outbreak of the second world war, it was closed as a student home. Though my stay at Arcadia was just a bit more than a year, there were some situations that occurred and which remain vivid in my memory and which I want to share. The first incident took place on a Sunday afternoon when things were fairly quiet. A few of us decided to play hide and seek — a game most kids play, and it's a wonderful way to pass the time. The problem developed when we decided to play in an area that was "off limits". It was the section of the barn where we kept the horses. Foolishly, I tried to sneak into the stall with one of the horses. I quickly learned that you don't approach a horse from behind without giving notice! The horse threw a heavy kick my way, and fortunately only caught my heel; but unfortunately, the kick was so swift that it left me with a heel swollen the size of an orange. To report it to the housefather would have gotten me some nice demerits for being where I should not have been, so the only option open to me was to bear the pain and keep my mouth shut. In later years, this injury would come back to haunt me.

On the farm summer's end meant that the silos had to be filled. Making hay and even shocking

Eva, Andy, June (Jack's wife), and Minerva.

... a rare occasion when seven of the eight were together. Front: Clark, Albert, and Minerva. Back: Eva, Betty, Andy, and Jack.

Front: Andy. Back: Minerva, Jack, and Betty.

wheat were not very high on my list of things I enjoyed doing, but certainly at the bottom of that list was filling the silo. It was a smelly, unpleasant task because we went into the silo while the insulage was being blown in. Our mission was to tromp (pack) the silage. The job didn't take an hour or so, it was an all day job. When the silo was filled and we were given the signal, we made a dash for the showers.

The younger boys did housework while the older ones went out each morning and evening to do the milking. An average herd numbered about thirty-two Holsteins. Housework involved doing dishes, setting the tables, shining the floors, washing the windows, sweeping the porches, etc. Each boy was responsible for making his bed and keeping his closet and drawers in good order. The older boys went to the barn. Cows had to be curried, manure had to be scooped and transported to the pit, the cows needed to be fed and just about the time that you thought there was nothing to do, the housefather had a list a mile long. For some reason, within a couple of months on the farm, I was sent to the barn. Wow, for a neophyte, that was status! Learning to milk was not difficult, but one of the older boys was instructed to supervise me to insure that the milking was done properly. However, it didn't take me long to manage the process by myself.

The first year on the farm passed rapidly. It wasn't long until we had the arrival of some new guys (sixth graders) which meant that Dick and I were enjoying upward mobility. Now we were in the seventh grade; we were gaining status not only on the farm but also on "The Hill."

A December day in 1941 remains vivid in my memory. It was Sunday, and some of us were lying on the floor in front of the radio. It was late afternoon when the news interrupted our program: "Pearl Harbor was under attack by Japan." Our nation's president called that Sunday "a day of infamy."

Because of the war and in the spring of 1941, farm home Arcadia was closed and would never again be used as a student home. Distance, with gas rationing and all that it implied, necessitated this action. So, once again, my bags were packed and off to a new farm home I went. I was the only Arcadian who was sent to Willow Wood. Perhaps, the boys were singularly distributed so that the farms to which they were sent could easily assimilate them.

In the summer of 1941 my brother Albert moved from the cottage to the farm, and he was assigned to be with me at Willow Wood. It was the first time that he and I would live under the same roof since our mother's death five years earlier. Of course, we saw each other on Sunday at chapel and on other occasions when the entire student body was brought together. Also, the proximity of Willow Wood to "The Main" made it possible for me through the spring and early summer to secure visitation privileges.

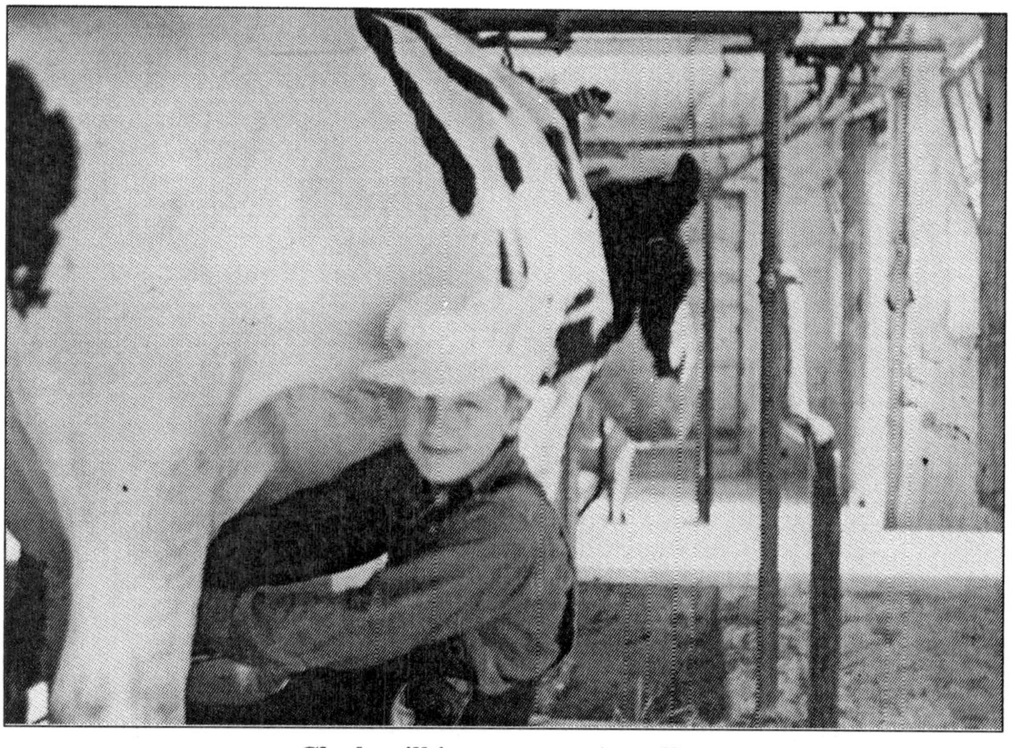

Clark milking a cow at Arcadia.

At Willow Wood, my houseparents were good people. At this point in the school's history, houseparents on the farm were generally employed on the basis of their ability to manage a farm. I believe it would be fair to say that only a few had depth of understanding regarding adolescent boys. It would also be fair to say that given their lack of understanding in this area, most of them did a pretty good job. Those who did not were soon "weeded" out. Fortunately, the houseparents had supervisors who possessed great expertise to whom they could turn for advice — especially when it came to discipline. While it is rarely discussed, there were those rare occasions when a housefather would, literally, tangle with a student(s). On two occasions, I witnessed it.

A year after I arrived at Willow Wood, the houseparents in charge resigned. This was a disappointment to me because I had a good relationship especially with this housefather. A new set of "in charge" houseparents were sent to us. They came from another farm home which meant that they had experience and were ready to take up where the others had left off. Each farm home had a second set of houseparents who were in a supporting role; most were being groomed with the hope of one day being in charge of their own farm home. The "second help," as we called them, were not the disciplinarians and made few, if any, of the decisions. To be honest about it, they were the popular ones; they were easier to get along with and were usually more patient with the boys. They were more lenient with us.

A wonderful young couple came to Willow Wood in this supportive role. We really appreciated them because they were kind and compassionate people. They viewed their job as a "calling." This housefather was working on his bachelor's degree at a nearby college with the dream of becoming a school teacher. He and his wife were with us a relatively short time.

One morning we got up, put on our milking suits, went down to the barn and discovered that the "second help" was in charge, and for the whole day! It started out like a normal day; and all went well with the milking. We ate breakfast and then dressed for school. The bus was on time. That afternoon when we returned from school, we dutifully went about the business of chores. Those of us who had barn chores were well aware of the absence of our housefather, but we knew what had to be done and we did it. With the work completed, we headed for the house, changed clothes, and waited for the bell to summon us to the dining room. Our housemother was noticeably quiet. We didn't know what was happening, and, exercising discretion, we didn't raise any questions. After our evening meal, those responsible to do so took care of the dishes and the related house work.

We all sensed something was wrong. Monday through Friday we were required to spend an hour on our studies. Talking was not permitted; the housefather carefully supervised the study period. This particular evening, we were about fifteen minutes into the study hour when our housemother came into the room. She was obviously shaken and distressed. She looked to one of the older boys asking him if he would lead a search for her husband. She told us that he had eaten lunch with her, after which he had gone out to do some work. Since then, she hadn't seen him and feared that something had happened to him. We all joined the search. We looked everywhere in and around the barn, but there was no sign of him. Then a few of us went up to the corn barn: a building that stood within yards of where the bus had dropped us off. With flashlights we went into this building, and there we found him. He had been up above doing some work and fell through the opening to the floor below. He was lifeless. What a tragedy! He was such a kind and good young man with great potential. He and his wife, like so many of the administrators, teachers, and houseparents, were people of great faith. The boys who lived at Willow Wood attended our house-father's funeral. It was held in his church at Annville, PA., a town near Hershey.

Farm Home Willow Wood consistently fielded good baseball teams. In the study room (living room), a number of pennants draped the walls, hopefully an inspiration to the younger boys. The farm homes

Farm Home Willow Wood

dotted the countryside and surrounded the town of Hershey. Many of the homes were in good proximity to others creating a natural "league" for competitive sports such as baseball and football. Willow Wood took its share of championships in baseball.

Summer was not just a time to work on the farm. There was plenty of spare time given to play. Farm homes competing in athletics not only used up the energy of the boys but also provided opportunity for many of them to participate. Baseball was the main intra-farm home sport, but the boys of Willow Wood also enjoyed an annual Thanksgiving tackle football (no pads) game against our arch rival, Farm 40. I'm certain that the houseparents at both farms were unaware of this "classic" event because it was inconceivable that they would give consent to such risky business.

The years that I spent at Willow Wood opened the door for me to enjoy some terrific housebrothers. Some were closer to me than others because of age, interests and personality. At Willow Wood, I established friendships that have endured. We shared experiences that neither time nor death can erase.

One day a new boy arrived from Philadelphia and was assigned to our farm home. He became the fourth boy in our bedroom. That first night, after we said our bedside prayers , lights were turned out and we were ready to sleep, the "new guy" opened his window wide, took a big breath and exhaling, said, "Oh, this great country air!" At that moment, he

Willow Wood Boys during study hour.

was the target of three pillows that were thrown his way. That good country air was scented with newly-spread manure.

When lights were out, it was assumed that the boys would roll over and go to sleep. That was not always the case. After the boys had reached fifteen or sixteen years of age, they naturally became adventurous. We called it "hooking out." Quietly, we would lie in bed until we were certain that the housefather had completed bed check; when the door of his apartment closed, out of our beds we would leap. We developed the art of slipping down the stairs avoiding those stair treads that squeaked. A little piece of wood in the proper place insured that the door could easily be reentered upon our return. Once outside, we would put on the shoes that we wisely carried while making our departure. If the moon was lighting up the night, care had to be taken as we silently and quickly made our way across the lawn, taking advantage of trees. Fortunately, we had a cherry orchard at Willow Wood which provided excellent cover on these rare occasions. In late summer and early autumn, the cornfields were also our allies when "hooking out.

What did we do when we got to town? There were various options, depending on the time of year. From Memorial Day to Labor Day, Hersheypark with all of its lights and activity beckoned us. In the winter, there were hockey games, and it was surprising how easily you could pick up a free ticket from some generous soul. If one was fortunate to have a girlfriend, her home definitely was a destination.

While in my high school years, I dated a girl who lived in town whose parents were very welcoming to not only me but all of my buddies as well. When visiting there, we were assured of having a nice supply of soda and pretzels.

Bob and Jim, my usual companions on such excursions, were always able to enjoy our time away. Somehow, God must have given me an overdose of conscience; it was hard for me to enjoy myself, and I was never comfortable until we were back in our beds. These extra-curricular escapades were well planned and not too frequent. We were wise enough to know that one should not push his luck.

Our closest brush with "exposure" happened this way:

During the second world war, many people doubled-up for the sake of the war effort. Our housefather worked at night in the chocolate factory. This made "hooking out" a safer bet. However, one evening as we sauntered down the sidewalk past the department store on our way to Hersheypark guess who was parked, facing the side of the store and facing three young men who were having the time of their lives? Yes, it was our housefather who was sitting in the driver's seat of his auto. We were caught...or were we? He must have been snoozing, waiting for his shift to begin. For days, we sweated it out, not knowing when or how he would confront us with this infraction of the rules. He was not one to say, "Oh well, boys will be boys." If, indeed, he saw us, without question he would have found great delight in rewarding us with demerits. The days passed, and then weeks passed; eventually, we concluded that miraculously, we had escaped detection. That experience slowed down our activity in this regard. From that point on, we limited our get-aways to Saturday or Sunday afternoon, when we could conjure up some excuse to be unreachable for a couple of hours. Willow Wood was just a hop, skip, and a jump from town. Palmdale was one of the points of interest because it happened to be the place where Bob's girlfriend lived. It was also easily accessible. We crossed the fish hatchery, climbed the hill, walked past a student home, Overview, and then it was just a short distance down the lane that ran adjacent to the golf course.

Accruing more than my share of demerits for other reasons, I put a halt to my participation in these unauthorized excursions. While we were gone, I kept saying to my buddies, "What if we get caught?" "Are we going to get away with this?" Bob would laugh and say, "Shug, when the good Lord passed out consciences, he gave you an overdose." Fortunately, I was caught only once and once was enough!

When we reached the upper grades, learning to socialize with the opposite sex was important. Remember, at this time, "The Home" was an all male institution; we were not accustomed to having girls around...we learned about them as we dated them.

Willow Wood Boys dining.

In an attempt to facilitate social skills, we were permitted farm home parties. At Willow Wood the older guys brought invited guests, and the party that I specifically remember was held at Halloween.

For weeks, the party was at the heart of our discussions. "Whom are you inviting? Have you asked her yet?" At that point in time, I had my eye on a lovely young lady who happened to be the drum majorette of the Hershey High School band. I had gotten to know her in what I called a "professional" way. I was the drum major of our school's band. There were some occasions when our bands marched in the same parades, and this opened the door for me to talk with and get to know this young lady. After spending days agonizing over how I would ask her to the farm home party, I just did it — and she accepted. However, what at first seemed to be a great opportunity ended in disaster. During the course of the evening, somehow one of my fairly good buddies managed to "steal" my date. He ended up taking her home. While I was devastated, I outwardly assured my housebrother that it was okay. That experience taught me the fickleness of females, and it took a long time before I was ready to risk rejection once more...like a week or so!

A genuine rivalry existed between The Homeboys and Hershey High School public students as we vied for the affection of the young women in town. This rivalry carried over into the arena of sports. When a

Homeboy dated a girl steadily, it was not uncommon to create a fuss that caused a temporary break-up prior to Christmas or her birthday due to a lack of funds to purchase the girl a gift. After the special event had passed, one could safely make amends and renew the relationship.

On the farm there were plenty of chores to go around. Milking was something that would never go away, and in the spring/early summer, there was corn to hoe. Through the summer weeks, we made hay and harvested wheat and/or barley which first had to be shocked. In the fall we became corn huskers after revealing our ability to set up some sturdy corn shocks.

The housefather selected me as one who would work with the teams. At Willow Wood, we had a team of mules, Fanny and Maggie, and we had a team of work horses, Charlie and Jerry. In my junior year, I spent many hours in the corn field with the mules cultivating. It was something that I thoroughly enjoyed. Working with the teams involved getting them, returning them, and caring for them. We shared a horse barn with farm home, Overview. Each farm was responsible for taking care of its own horses and/or mules. I enjoyed this work because it minimized the amount of milking that I had to do.

One morning in the dining room while eating breakfast, a younger boy who sat at my table had a problem. His nose was running and he needed to excuse himself from the table and go into the hallway to blow his nose. I took it upon myself to tell him. He just sat there sniffling and irritating the rest of us. He asked for a second helping of pancakes; I said, "No, not until you go and blow your nose." Keep in mind that I was not entrusted with the authority to say and do what I did, but I usurped authority, thinking that I was being a good mentor. Stubbornly, the boy said, "No! Please pass me the pancakes." Once more, I said, "Not until you leave the table, blow your snotty nose, and quit ruining our appetites." The boy wouldn't comply, and he didn't get what he asked for, namely the pancakes. It made me look bad; no question about it.

What happened? The housefather reported me, and I promptly had a visit from the Dean of Students. The report listed me as having been abusive to a younger boy, something that I would never have done. I thought that I was being a responsible, older boy; from the housefather's perspective, I was getting "too big for my britches." A day or two later, the Dean of Students came to Willow Wood to resolve the situation. He was genuinely kind and keenly sensitive to what was happening. He had been a housefather when he began employment with "The Home," so he knew the kinds of things that go on within the context of a farm home life. He invited me to sit with him in his automobile. He sat in the driver's seat, which, incidentally, was a nice bit of symbolism, and I sat in the passenger's seat. He spared me the embarrassment of being taken to task in front of the other boys, but even more importantly, he lectured me and "dished out" the demerits without the housefather being present. The presence of the housefather would have been devastating to me. Yes, I did get demerits, but the way the situation was handled enabled all to come through it with their dignity in tact.

This Dean of Students (Dr. John O. Hershey) eventually became the president of this unique institution providing it with strong, prudent leadership for many years. He also became a very important influence in my life. Through the years he has become a valued friend and confidant; he is one to whom I could turn and know that he genuinely cared not only about me but about all of the graduates after they had left "The Home."

Willow Wood was my home for five and a half of the eleven years that I spent in "The Home." It was a good home: in a good location and good from the standpoint of the students with whom I was privileged to live. Many of the boys talked, with affection, about their houseparents. At Willow Wood, our "first help" did not relate well to some of the boys in his charge. He was in charge and used every opportunity to hammer that reality home. I feel confident that he cared about us, in his own way but if that was the case, the message didn't come shining through. However, we did enjoy some genuinely caring houseparents who were in the supporting or backup role.

Having my younger brother with me at Willow Wood enabled us to enter into various activities together. He and I shared a very close relationship. In fact, one of the older boys told me that our relationship as brothers was weird! We didn't argue or get into the typical scuffles often associated with siblings.

One Sunday afternoon, the two of us felt the urge to have a snack. The problem? At our farm home, except for meal time, the pantry was "off limits." As brother Albert and I reasoned the situation, we concurred that everything in the pantry belonged to "The Home," and "The Home" existed to take care of the boys, so that would surely mean whatever we found on the pantry shelves belonged to us. You can't "steal" it, if, in effect, it belongs to you. An interesting theology, wouldn't you say? After discussing to whom the pantry's contents belonged, we moved on to formulate a plan by which we could "acquire" what belonged to us. This was the plan: I was to be the look-out. If I saw anything suspicious (like the housefather coming our way), it would be my responsibility to alert brother Albert. He would be busy looking for something worthy of the risk that we were taking. The way it turned out, the only available snack was a box of raisins, and neither of us cared much for them. However, as Albert was diligently raiding the pantry shelves, I heard the shuffling of slippers, and I knew who was coming. Before I could warn my brother, the housefather appeared on the scene catching Albert with his hand in the raisin box. The housefather was livid, and as he pounded my little brother, verbally, he began a search for me. He knew if one of us was there, the other would be also. By this time, I managed to squeeze between the refrigerator and the wall. He was a great "investigator," and it took him only a matter of seconds to find me. He sent us to our bedroom where he would meet us, and we knew there was going to be a price to pay. Our housefather was a big man; he was strong and knew how to use a paddle. We wore welts for days to come. Unscheduled visits to the pantry were no longer of interest to us.

On a more positive note, my brother and I decided that we would try our skill at trapping. Willow Wood not only had a spring creek passing through its pasture, but it also had a fish hatchery; both made it a natural for trapping enthusiasts. One morning, when Albert was out checking our traps, he discovered that we had gotten a skunk. Not too familiar with skunks and their main line of defense, he returned to the house doused with skunk perfume. He was immediately sent out into the field with very specific instructions: "Bury those clothes!" We all learned a lesson, at Albert's expense. In future encounters with skunks, we kept our distance and we were very careful how we approached them!

Birthdays were always special at "The Home." A cake was sent out to the student home in which a boy was enjoying a birthday; the cake would be shared with all of his housebrothers. I remember my sixteenth birthday; not only was there a cake, but the sixteenth birthday also brought an increase in allowance and one night out to town every week. Plus one received a lapel pin marking the sixteenth birthday. The pin had on it a wreath and a keystone, the latter being the emblem of Pennsylvania. Prominently displayed were the initials of H.I.S. The pin was in the school's colors of brown and gold.

On the farm, we lived as a family. There were happy times, and there were difficult times. But when the chips were down, we pulled together. When new boys arrived, it didn't take them long to feel that they belonged. In the spring of the year, the seniors looked forward to graduation and getting "out on their own." We celebrated with them and shared their joy, but it was also sad to say goodbye to brothers with whom we had shared so intimately. In some strange and wonderful way, no matter where they went or how long ago they left, we'd always be connected. We were Homeboys...we are family.

VI.
ON THE RUN

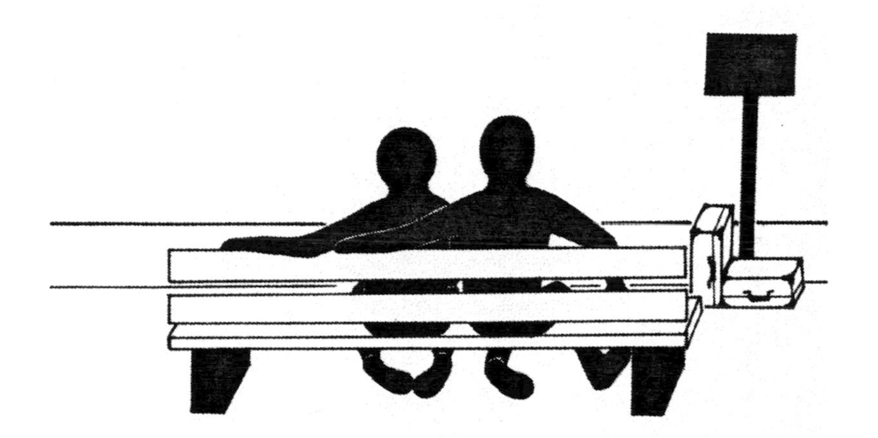

Why would a Homeboy run away? If you gained a large family, have good food and the opportunity to receive a good education, why would anyone run from it?

When I was in the sixth grade, I ran away with one of my former Kinderhaus buddies. This happened the first year that I was on the farm. At Arcadia, the farm home, we had a bully in the home who took great delight in making life miserable for me. Running from the problem seemed easier than staying. To go to the housefather and report "the bully" was not an acceptable option. The boy who ran away with me was also having some adjustment problems at his farm home. He was a native of Harrisburg, so because of its close proximity, we decided to go there. I'm not sure what we thought we would do once we got to Harrisburg, but that was our destination. With no bus money, we hitch-hiked to downtown Harrisburg. It was winter and soon we were cold and hungry. My buddy telephoned a relative of his who immediately picked us up and chauffeured us back to our respective farm homes. That brought to an end the first of three "runs," an activity that earned me the title of, "The Run Away Kid."

The second incident occurred a little more than a year later. I was well on my way to finishing seventh grade. My younger brother, Albert, was completing the fifth grade. He was still in the junior division living at "The Main" at Kinderhaus where I had lived prior to going to the farm. It was on a Sunday morning after we had been to chapel that we "disappeared." I didn't board the bus for Willow Wood, and Albert didn't get on the trolley for the short trip back to Kinderhaus. Albert's housemother must have been frantic wondering what had happened to him. I've always felt badly about the pain that I was responsible for causing her.

Hand in hand, the two of us started walking in the direction of Harrisburg. After thinking that we had covered a lot of ground, we went up to a farm house and knocked on the door. To the man who appeared and opened the door, I said, "Mister, do you need a hired hand? I can milk cows, and I am capable of doing other farm work. If you will let my brother and me stay here, I'll work for you." When the man first laid eyes on us, he surely knew that we were Homeboys. We didn't wear uniforms, but we wore good clothing. The people in the area could spot a Homeboy from a mile away, simply by the way he was dressed. The farmer, however, played along with us. His response was, "Just the other day, I told my wife that I needed to hire some help for the farm. Come on in." The afternoon was spent with us playing with the farmer's children. About four in the afternoon, I happened to look out the window and spotted a state police car coming up the drive. In that moment, I knew the jig was up!

We were greeted by the two troopers who informed us that they had come to take us back to "The

Home." Obviously, the farmer put in a call to the state police when we were distracted. The troopers asked us if we would like to join them for the evening meal at the barracks. Pennsylvania State Troopers while in training lived together at the barracks much like soldiers when undergoing basic training. Before dinner that evening, they took us out to see the horses. We were given a tour of the barracks, and then it was time to sit down at the tables and eat. That was quite an experience. When we finished eating, they first took Albert over to Kinderhaus, after which they dropped me off at Willow Wood. Before I got out of the car, they talked seriously to me concerning the danger in which my brother and I placed ourselves: walking along the highway and then approaching people whom we didn't know. They made me promise that I wouldn't run away again. I promised, and I didn't run away until a year or more later.

The third and final escapade occurred as I was nearing my eighth grade year and Albert was finishing sixth grade. While we were on vacation the previous summer, an aunt (a sister to our mother) had taken the two of us for a sundae. As we enjoyed this treat, she told us how much she loved us and that if we ever wanted to live with her, she would take us in. She should not have said this because she didn't really mean it. We foolishly believed her.

When our two weeks at McKeesport ended and we were returning from vacation, the words of our aunt continued to ring in my ears. She was telling us that she wanted us to live with her, I thought! By this time, both Albert and I were students at Willow Wood. There was plenty of time for us to talk about how differently things could be if we lived with our aunt. It wasn't long until we developed a plan. This time we had suitcases. We actually believed that our aunt wanted us to live with her. Once more, we headed west. We hitch-hiked to Harrisburg to the train station. I said to my brother, "Sit there and keep a close eye on our suitcases." In the meantime, I took my place in line, and by the time I reached the ticket window, a wonderful lady in front of me had been persuaded to buy two young boys tickets to Pittsburgh.What I told the woman, I cannot remember, but I must have been convincing because I was successful. The second World War was still on. Women and military personnel had priority on the seats. Albert and I sat on our suitcases in the aisle all the way from Harrisburg to Pittsburgh, some two hundred miles.

Upon our arrival, I gave Albert the same instructions, "Sit there and watch our suitcases." Off I went in search of some benevolent soul who could be convinced to give me money for a phone call. It didn't take long at all to find such a person. Can you imagine the shock of my aunt when she heard a cheerful voice on the other end saying, "Aunt Minerva, this is Clark. Albert and I are here at the train station in Pittsburgh. We're taking you up on your offer to have us live with you." "Hello...Aunt Minerva...are you there?" Yes, she was there, and she must have felt like she had been hit with a stun gun. She didn't know what to say. She was probably thinking about the phone call that she would have to make to our grandfather. Finally, after what seemed like an eternity, she gathered her composure and said, "Clark, you stay right there. I'll come over to Pittsburgh to get you." My brother and I sat patiently waiting, watching the people coming and going.

Eventually, I heard a man call our names: "Clark, Albert!" I jumped up thinking that our aunt had sent a friend. The man introduced himself and his partner to us; they were detectives with the Pittsburgh police department. They took us into custody and told us that we would be taken to the juvenile detention center. Our grandfather, the retired policeman, who lived only twenty to thirty minutes away was determined to teach us a lesson. We were picked up at the train station on Friday night, and we were kept at the detention center until Monday morning. It was a frightening experience. There were bars on the windows. They took our clothes from us and gave us one piece coveralls to wear. At night, all the boys slept in this large room on cots. Fortunately, my brother and I were able to stay together. Many of the kids who were in this detention center had street experience. Albert and I kept to ourselves.

Back when I was sent off to Hershey, I felt that the family had abandoned me, and now I felt that they had betrayed my brother and me. Why didn't someone come? Already we were becoming homesick for "The Home." Saturday was a long day for us, wondering when we would get out. On Sunday morning, the chaplain offered to give any kid a New Testament if he could recite one of the Psalms. With our religious training at Hershey, that was a piece of cake for Albert and me. We each recited a Psalm, and we were each given a New Testament. Finally on Monday morning, our grandfather arrived to arrange for our release. He was angrier than a hornet. All the way to McKeesport (about fifteen miles), he lectured us.

Fortunately for him, my brother went off with Aunt Eva (his guardian); I had to stay with my grandparents, and occasionally I would get a lecture on how wonderful I had it at the Hershey Industrial School. Grandfather was right! I couldn't have agreed with him more. As soon as all the arrangements could be made, my brother and I were placed on a Greyhound bus headed for Harrisburg. One of the employees of the school met us and returned us to Willow Wood. Frankly, we were thrilled to be back, and that was the last time that running away was ever discussed. It was good to be back with our buddies; now we knew where we belonged.

Why does one run away from a place like Hershey? Maybe it is in search of an answer to the question, "Where do I belong?"

VII.
ON THE HILL

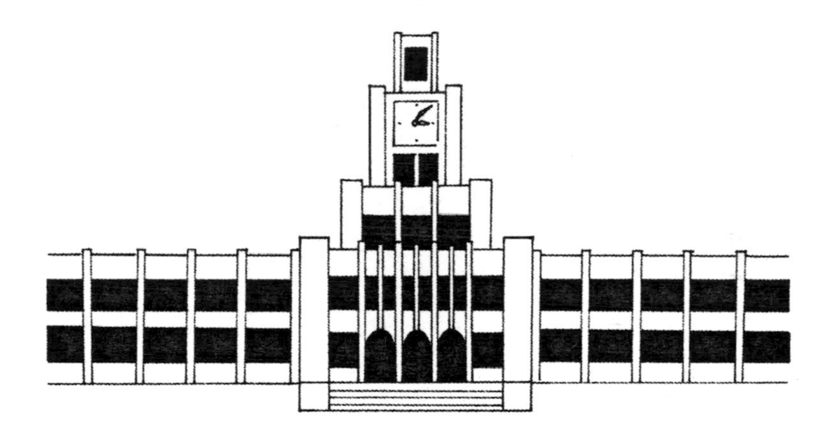

Going to "The Hill" was something to shout about; it was something to which we looked forward throughout the fifth grade. I'm sure that most of us experienced some anxiety as well as excitement because it also meant that we would be leaving the cottages and going out to live on the farm. It wasn't just a matter of changing schools; we were also changing home life. In a way, it was like a rite of passage. We were no longer going to be "kids"; we would be young men in the making and that would imply more responsibility.

When I went to "The Hill," as we called it, I was starting my fifth year in "The Home." Some of the boys who eventually graduated with me (the class of 1947) had not yet become Homeboys. The School admitted boys between the ages of four and fourteen. The upper age was set premised on the thinking that after age fourteen, one would not be in the school long enough to benefit from all that it offered.

Going to "The Hill" also meant that we would be with the "big guys." While we were at "The Main," it was a rare occasion for all the boys to be in one place at the same time. Now we would not only see our "heroes," but there would be the opportunity to speak with them and to live with some of them.

Why did we refer to the Junior-Senior High School as "The Hill"? Because it sits very majestically, high on Patt's Hill, overlooking the town of Hershey. At football games when we were seated in the stadium on the home team's side looking up and to our left, we would see this magnificent specimen of architecture looking down upon us. It is a landmark. Under its roof were thirteen shops — the trades were offered to those students who were not headed for college. From its front perspective, the administrative area with an impressive clock-tower provided an attractive entrance; to the east was the junior high wing and to the west was the senior high wing.

Transportation to "The Hill" from the more than sixty farm homes was by bus. The campus which included the farms embraces some ten thousand acres. The farm homes dotted the countryside around the town of Hershey. Each morning, Monday through Friday, the buses rolled, delivering the boys from near and far for classes that began at 9:00 a.m.

Things on "The Hill" were quite different from what we had become accustomed to down at "The Main." Listing them brings them to the fore:

- No longer would we walk from our places of residence to class; we had to rely on bus transportation.

- Most of the teachers on "The Hill" were men; at "The Main," they were mostly women.

- The Junior-Senior High School was huge with a lot of areas to explore.

Jr-Sr High School overlooking the town.

• At "The Main," those of us in the fifth grade knew just about all of the other students; on "The Hill," we would only know some of the seventh and eighth graders who in previous years had been with us at "The Main."

The first day on "The Hill" was, indeed, an intriguing experience. One needed a map to find his way around. The impressive fourteen hundred seat auditorium is awesome! While it is true that Fanny B. Memorial (The Main) had an auditorium and swimming pool, they didn't hold a candle to the auditorium and swimming pool on "The Hill." The big gym and mammoth cafeteria were genuinely intimidating to us.

In light of all the changes, those early weeks of sixth grade required a lot of adjusting. But we were Homeboys, and we took it all in stride!

Now that I was on the farm and attending classes on "The Hill" like my peers, I took more interest in attending football and basketball games. After school, while waiting for the bus, I would watch the teams (in season) practicing. Our athletes became the heroes whom we younger boys emulated. We even collected their autographs. I was so profoundly impressed with them, I've never forgotten what they inscribed in my autograph book. One of them wrote:

"I thought, I thought, I thought in vain,
so I thought I'd write my name."
(He then signed his name.)

Another of my "heroes" scribbled the following into my book:

"Good, better, best. Always do your best.
When your good is better, then your better best."
(He signed his name.)

I was so impressed with those "heroes" that through all these years, I've not forgotten what they put on paper for me. Their method of signing an autograph reflected character and maturity.

Academics, athletics, music, and the arts were all emphasized as important to our development. Early in my sixth grade year, I decided on violin lessons. My enthusiasm for this instrument was short lived. It required the kind of discipline that I was not up to accepting. Soon, I found it a bit boring. On one occasion, during a lesson with three other hopefuls, we were playing our lesson accompanied on the piano by the teacher. When we arrived at the end of the piece, I quickly dropped to my seat; the other boys did the same. "Come on boys...get on your feet and let's run over that once more," the teacher said. Reluctantly and with an audible sigh, I got to my feet. The music teacher said, "Clark, you may lay down your instrument and be excused." That brought my violin lessons to an abrupt end.

But there is life after violin lessons. I somehow knew that the drum was my instrument. This teacher was the band director and he became a very important person in my life. He was the clone of John Philip Sousa, even to the pinch-on glasses. He was truly a master musician and one who wasn't willing to tolerate "tom foolery." I didn't do badly with drum lessons, but I became impatient. I tired of beating on a rubber pad; I wanted a real drum. Too soon and foolishly, I dropped out of drum lessons.

With the passage of time, it became apparent to me that I was meant to be a pianist, so I enrolled as a piano student. I lasted longer with the piano than with the other two instruments, but again, I lacked the dedication required of one who would enjoy significant progress. A wise teacher told me, "Clark, you want to pick the fruit without planting the tree!" At that time, I didn't get it, but I do now.

Back to the band director. He was truly influential in my life. In fact, he became my father-confessor. When I had a problem (and it seemed that my life was full of them), I looked him up; he listened to me, but he was also firm with me. He didn't hesitate to tell me what I needed to hear. However, he did it in a fatherly way which kept me going back to him, to lean on him.

Another teacher, in those years from sixth grade through my senior year, who was a big influence in my life was my piano teacher. He was young, just beginning his teaching career, while the band director was older and within a decade of retirement. Both of these music teachers were persons in whom I felt comfortable confiding.

While I have to be honest and confess that my studies were not given the time they deserved, on

The Glee Club (Clark in back row, 5th from right).

the other hand, I invested heavily in extracurricular activities. I sang with the Choir, the Glee Club, and in my senior year, the Octet. The Choir and Glee Club sang regularly at chapel services. Beyond that, the Glee Club was involved in numerous activities: forensic competition (we were state champs in my senior year), concerts at various churches in central Pennsylvania, and occasionally we engaged in exchange programs with other regional high schools. An annual event and high point of the year for the Glee Club was its spring concert held on "The Hill" for both the student body and interested friends. It was always an emotional concert because for the seniors, this was their "swan song."

The out of town concerts were especially enjoyable. We visited churches in nearby communities, and our means of travel was the regular school bus. Always we would sing as we traveled. Some of the songs were "fun" things while others were part of our repertoire.

One Sunday evening as we were returning from a distant concert, rolling down the highway we were singing "Pop Goes the Weasel." Just as we sang "pop," a tire blew out, leaving us along the side of the road until a repair truck arrived. This incident left us with something to talk and laugh about for weeks "down the road."

Other extracurricular activities in which I was involved and which required a nice investment of time included:

(a) Football - as a freshman, I played half-back and enjoyed football; however, an injury caused the school's doctor to advise me to refrain from future participation in this "contact sport."
(b) I became Drum Major of the Band; this insured my being able to attend all the football games, including those that were away. Also, there were many parades for which to prepare (Halloween, Memorial Day, etc.). These parades took us to a number of communities outside of Hershey.
(c) Like most of the boys, I was heavily into intramural sports; this consisted mainly of basketball, softball, and baseball (at the farm home). There was a nice sense of competition that existed between the various shops on "The Hill." There was also a healthy sense of competition between farm home clusters.

After completing the ninth grade, Homeboys were ready to move into the senior high division; for some, that meant the college preparation course, but for others it meant the commercial course of study to prepare for the business world (bookkeeping, shorthand, and other skills needed to work in a bank or office).

The vast majority of students entered the trades. Our shops had instructors of high quality, and the

The Homeboy as Drum Major.

shops were equipped with the best tools and equipment available.

Toward the end of the school year, the entire freshman class met in the auditorium to hear the announcement of curriculum assignments. The administrators did their best to place a student in his first choice...however, for practical and other reasons, this wasn't always possible. Some of the boys had to settle for their second choice. Initially, I started out in the commercial course, but shortly thereafter, I transferred to the carpentry shop. While I didn't follow this trade after graduation (nor did I develop into a terrific carpenter), what I learned in that course of study became very useful throughout my professional life.

We alternated with two weeks in class and then two weeks in shop. This arrangement proved to be highly effective. While many of the graduates didn't continue in their trade after high school, the fact remains each student was given a wonderful foundation upon which to build. It is interesting to note that a large number of shop students after graduation went on to college and entered the professions. Homeboys had instilled in them a strong work ethic.

On "The Hill," many clubs and organizations were open to the boys to supplement and enhance their study programs. The Christian Knights (the Homeboys' version of a church's youth group), Boy

Scouts, Photography Club, Drama Club, and a number of other such clubs were popular among the students. One club which didn't require an official joining was the Dance Club. After lunch, those of us who were interested in developing or improving dancing skills just "showed up." Since it was an all boys' school, we had to do our learning and/or improving by dancing with other boys. We didn't feel uncomfortable with this arrangement; actually, we had no alternative. We were Homeboys! Many of us became fairly proficient dancers. When we attended social functions and had occasion to dance with female partners, it was then that we could fully appreciate our "brothers" whose instruction and assistance helped us develop enviable dancing skills.

There are many experiences from "The Hill" which remain vivid in my collection of memories. In my first year up at the Junior-Senior High School, our nation was drawn into World War II. This meant that more and more Homeboys who had graduated and were graduating entered the armed forces. It was a thrill for us to see alumni walking those hallowed corridors in uniform which many of them did. Often prior to their departure for overseas duty, alumni would return "home" to see the people whom they considered family and the place which they considered home.

During the war years, at Friday afternoon assemblies, our beloved principal, W. Allen Hammond, would share portions of letters which he received from Homeboys who were at various levels of their training at bases around the country. As the war went on, these letters would come from bases overseas. In assembly on "The Hill," we listened intently and had great respect for our H.I.S. brothers who were serving Uncle Sam. Of course, there were those sad occasions when reports arrived and were shared with the student body of alumni killed in action and/or were missing in action. We heard about those who were taken as prisoners of war; they were in our prayers. A number of these alumni were a decade or more ahead of us in school; their situation was extremely important to all of us because they and we were Homeboys...we were family.

Many of the alumni in the military were especially important to me because I remembered them playing varsity football, basketball and baseball. Some of them had been my housebrothers at Arcadia and later at Willow Wood. It is difficult to explain, but the fact remains, it doesn't matter when one graduated from this very special home/school, there is a unique bond that exists between alumni and between the alumni and the student body.

During the years of World War II, some of our teachers were called to bear arms; when they left, we missed them and then joyously celebrated their return to the faculty after the war's end.

When I was a sophomore in high school, as a member of the Glee Club, I participated in an event that I will never forget. Shortly before Christmas, 1944, the Glee Club went to the mansion, Highpoint, the home which Milton Hershey had built for his beloved Catherine, and our purpose was to sing Christmas carols for Milton S. Hershey. He stood at the top of the staircase; we sang from the mansion's entry area below. The ceiling was very high, providing us with good acoustics.

"M.S.", as we affectionately referred to him, said very little. From the top of the steps, he greeted us and made certain that there would be refreshments for us following our singing, but he did not come down the staircase to backslap or even shake our hands. We knew, however, that he was pleased with our singing. It showed by the sparkle in his eyes and the smile on his face. We left him that evening with a feeling that we had brightened his Christmas. At the time, we had no way of knowing that it would be his last Christmas because the following October, one month to the day after his 88th birthday, he passed through the valley of the shadow of death.

As a member of the Glee Club, I was privileged to be one of those who sang at the funeral of this great man, the Chocolate King, our foster father. The funeral was held in the auditorium of the Junior-Senior High School on "The Hill." His body lay in state in the foyer of the school. Clergy from the six churches in Hershey were in attendance at the service.

We, the Glee Club, sang two anthems: Bach's "Come, Those Sweet Death" and Malotte's arrangement of "The Lord's Prayer." Eight boys from the senior class were selected to carry the casket of our benefactor to its resting place. Mr. Hershey's body was laid to rest in the family burial plot up at Hershey Cemetery.

As I reflect on those memorable years which I spent on "The Hill," I must confess that academically I did not achieve the level of which I was capable. It wasn't a matter of inability, but it was one of difficulty focusing sharply on my studies. I did what I had to do to get by and nothing more. Often I have regretted not taking my studies more seriously. The day came when I realized the truth in those words spoken by a wise mentor:

"Life is God's gift to you and what you do with your life is your gift to God."

VIII.
ON A JOURNEY OF FAITH

Some years ago, a Lutheran Pastor friend of mine visited the Milton Hershey School and the first time that he saw me after this visit, he said, "Clark, you are right. 'The Home' in which you were raised is phenomenal. The moment that I set foot on its campus, I could sense an aura of spirituality."

Religion has always been an important component in the development of Homeboys. It began in the student home, continued in the classroom, and held a steady and firm position on the calendar. Every Sunday morning, each of the students, regardless of his religious preference, was required to attend chapel; a "general" Protestant format was used.

In the Deed of Trust, Milton Hershey stated that the school was to be "non-sectarian;" it was his intention that the religious training of his boys remain non-denominational. During the years that I was there, the student body was made up of Protestants, Roman Catholics, and Jews. When admitting a boy, his guardian understood that chapel attendance was compulsory. This was not an option; it was viewed as an essential ingredient in the strengthening of the moral and spiritual character of the students.

Milton Hershey's religious convictions were embodied in the Ten Commandments and the Golden Rule. While he was living, he insisted that both the Ten Commandments and the Golden Rule be displayed in each student home, and each student was issued a wallet-size copy of the Ten Commandments. It is important to note that the people whom Mr.

Hershey selected for leadership positions in his home/school were without exception individuals who openly embraced values consistent with Biblical principles. The day began with devotions. There was Scripture reading and prayer. It would have been unthinkable to eat a meal without first pausing to give thanks to Almighty God. In the evening before getting into bed, we were encouraged to kneel by our beds and say our prayers. This was a time when I especially thought about my grandmother Hobby who each evening, after reading her Bible, would kneel by her rocking chair to pray. At school the day began with prayer and the pledge of allegiance. Additionally, up through the eighth grade, there was a weekly class in religion (Bible).

I particularly remember our Bible teacher at the Fanny B. Memorial School. She taught us about the Cannanites, the Amalikites, the Jebusites, and a lot of other "ites", the details concerning whom we quickly forgot, but we never would forget the love for her Lord which she exuded. The administrators, faculty, houseparents and persons in supportive roles were persons of faith and strong character. Students were blessed with good, pious role models.

With this being said, I must confess that many times when I knelt for prayer, even in those early years, I wanted to scream at God and tell Him how angry I was at Him. I kept asking myself the question, "Why?" "Why did God take my parents from me? Why was I separated from my brothers and sisters and others of the family?"

I listened intently to my mentors as they spoke of God's love and providential care, but quietly I kept asking, "Why?" Interestingly, this was something that I never discussed with my buddies; I knew, as I am sure that they knew, each of us was bearing inward pain. Consequently, I don't think I dealt very well with my loss; the hurt and pain that I felt were manifested in my behavior. Maybe that is why I ran away and/or why at times I had difficulty with my housefather. Could I have been wanting someone to talk with me about my inner feelings?

When I talked with the faculty members whom I trusted and with whom I felt comfortable, the discussions always centered around my struggle in the classroom or my problems with my housefather. I avoided talking about what was really bothering me. The hurt and pain were so acute that only in recent years have I been able to openly discuss my early years of loss and separation. While it is true that during those early years I was quick to lay the blame at the doorstep of God, the fact remains that while I was unaware of it, God was wonderfully at work on my behalf. I needed to move on from loss so that I could recognize my gain. Indeed, I am convinced that it was by the providence of God that I was raised in the best home/school of its kind in the world. But it took time and the help of many people for me to appreciate the goodness of God in my life.

I tried to pay attention at chapel; some of the time it was easier than at other times. In my sophomore year, because of the influence of a female acquaintance, I began to attend a church in Hershey. I had great respect for its pastor. When World War II ended and our faculty members returned to their teaching positions, one of them was the director of the Glee Club. As a part time job, he served as the organist/choir director of the church that I was attending. He invited me to sing in his church choir, which I did.

At "The Home," I became involved with the Christian Knights, our version of a youth group. This organization facilitated Bible study and fellowship. This activity was helpful as I tried to resolve my personal struggle with God.

One day, the light of day broke through to me. I realized as never before that God was not at the source of my hurt and suffering. I reasoned it out in this way:

> It wasn't God who threw those canisters of mustard gas, causing my father and his comrades to be victims of chemical warfare. If I must lay some blame, I shouldn't be blaming God. I needed to blame the evilness of war and the hatefulness of humankind.
>
> Also, my mother's death came as a result of pneumonia and unfortunately prior to the era of miracle drugs. Her illness coupled with loneliness and deep grief caused by the loss of her husband took from her all desire to live.

The importance of my theological break-through was this: I put things in perspective and came to realize that God was for me and not, as I had supposed, against me. It was certainly heavy stuff for a young teenager. After this revelation, life became easier for me, and it was the start of getting my life on a more even keel. The proverbial "chip" was off my shoulder.

I don't want to minimize the help which came my way from the adults who interacted with me; and in a strange sort of way, I think my peers contributed significantly in this regard. In retrospect, I think it was rather profound theologizing for a lad in his early teens.

In about 1941 or '42, our chaplain resigned and was replaced with a science teacher who was given the title, "The Director of Religious Education." He was extremely effective in this role, and he went on to do graduate study while serving in this position. Mr. "B" was sensitive to my struggle. In one of our conversations, I told him that I often thought about my brother, Andy, and sisters, Minerva and Betty, who were at Scotland orphanage located some fifty miles west of Hershey near Chambersburg, PA. The opportunities to see and be with them were limited to two-week summer vacations, if and when the family arranged for vacations to McKeesport which was not every year.

One day Mr. "B" indicated that he wanted to see me after class. When the other boys had gone, he said to me, "Clark, I have arranged for you and your brother, Albert, to spend a weekend over at Scotland so that you can visit with your older brother and sisters." He took us on a Friday and returned us to our farm home Sunday evening. This incident is reflective of the interest that administrators and faculty (houseparents, too) had in the students. They deeply cared about us Homeboys, but at the same time they were limited as to what they were able to do.

The Scotland orphanage excursion proved to be a great experience for us. That weekend, five of the eight Hobby orphans were in one place at the same time which was a rare situation. It proved to be a memorable experience.

Mr. "B" soared toward the top of my list of persons with whom I could take my problems; I knew, without a doubt, that he would listen and that he really cared. Because of what he did, I developed a keen interest in Christian Knights and also volunteered to read lessons at the Sunday chapel services.

The summer between my junior and senior years, I was one of those who volunteered to teach Vacation Bible School. It was held for the young boys in the cottages at "The Main." For teaching, we were rewarded in two ways:

- The first reward came by way of the joy which we derived from teaching our little brothers.
- The second reward was in the form of permission to swim in the pool at "The Main" after each day's session.

What I didn't realize was the more enduring benefit for me personally. Teaching VBS further strengthened my own faith; it was another step on my journey of faith.

IX.
ON STAGE

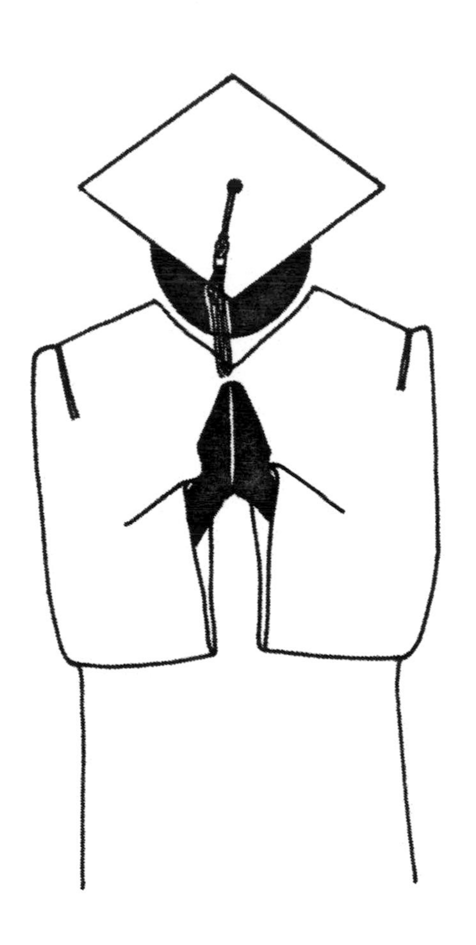

Being on stage wasn't something new for me. I had sung in the choir, and I was a four year member of the Glee Club. In my senior year I was a member of the Octet. For four years, I was in the marching band, and in my senior year, I was drum major. Additionally, as a junior in high school, I began to read the lessons at chapel services on a rotating basis. All of these activities frequently put me "on stage" if not literally then figuratively speaking.

However, the occasion that I want to share with you was very different; it was a unique experience and one that would not ever be repeated. I was on stage with my classmates anticipating receiving my diploma from a "world class" school. Each of us on the stage that night knew he was about to receive a document which represented not just achievement in the classroom but of life together. The Hershey Industrial School was first a home then a place of education, and that is what makes it so unique.

There on stage that graduation night as I looked around me, I saw young men who were not only my classmates but they were my "brothers," my family! The reality of being in that place (on stage) and the reason for being there began to sink in. Our senior year had passed too quickly. For years all that I wanted was to complete my senior year and be "free," but now that I was at that point in my life, it was scary. The only home that I actually remembered was my home at Hershey; I was a Homeboy, and "The Home" was my source of security. On stage, my thoughts raced back to the opening day of school the past September. We shouted with glee, "We are seniors!" We knew that each week as we walked those hallowed halls on "The Hill," we were going to experience a lot of last occasions. The last football season as Homeboys, the last Halloween, the last Thanksgiving Day, the last Christmas, and the list went on and on.

In the fall of the year, football was a sport that brought the entire student body together. The games were played in the big stadium which we shared with the local public school; the stadium was located over by Hersheypark. Our games were played Saturday afternoons. At the football games, the school spirit was quite impressive. The boys in the stands were directed and motivated by a group of male cheerleaders — remember, we had only boys enrolled in "The Home" at that time — and they displayed great support for our team. The cheers were punctuated with songs. The brisk, fall air was permeated with young voices as they sang:

"Onward Spartans, Onward Spartans, Onward to the fight..."

"O you can't stop the brown and gold..."

"Over hill, over dale...O, you can't stop the brown and gold!"

On and on, the boys would sing and cheer until the last minute on the clock ran out. We were Homeboys, and we stood solidly behind our "brothers" regardless of the numbers on the scoreboard.

It was a thrill for me, personally, to lead the band into the stadium prior to the game, and at the conclusion of thc prc-game ceremonies, marching off the field, I would throw the baton above the crossbar of the goal posts, catching it on the other side in stride. This was a tradition begun by predecessor drum majors. To miss catching the baton was viewed as an ominous omen regarding the game about to be played, so I made darn sure that I caught the baton as I strutted through the uprights of thc goal posts.

Concurrent with football games, there were parades in and out of town. Some of the surrounding communities would host Halloween parades, inviting high school bands plus drum and bugle corps along with variously sponsored floats to participate in the festivities. These were always enjoyable events. In the fall of the year, there were opportunities for the band to march in parades which were competitive in nature.

Also, the Glee Club was in high gear. We sang on Sunday evenings at different churches in and around central Pennsylvania. We not only provided inspiration/entertainment for those concert audiences, but we were also ambassadors of "The Home." Everywhere we went, people had heard of Hershey bars, but most were totally unaware of the magnificent home/school which had been founded by the chocolate magnate: M.S. Hershey.

Whether a football player, a Band member, or one of the Glee Clubbers, one took seriously the opportunity, and privilege, of representing the Hershey Industrial School. We took great pride in who we were and "The Home" that we were representing.

In my senior year, the Glee Club traveled to Washington, D.C., to give a concert. Can you imagine the excitement that was ours? Many of us had never been anywhere other than the trip back to our places of origin for a two-week vacation. In my case, this meant a ride on the Greyhound bus which left Harrisburg, picking up the Pennsylvania turnpike at Carlisle, which ended at Irwin. It was then on to East McKeesport where the driver would supervise the disembarking of my brother and me. A family member would be there to meet us. That was the extent of my travels up to this point in my life, so the Washington engagement was my first time out of the state of Pennsylvania.

Lodging was arranged by school officials. One of my buddies, Bob H., was originally from Washington; he was going to be staying with his mother, and I was invited to stay there, too. He, another boy, and I rode with the Glee Club director in his auto rather than riding the bus. He dropped us off at the train station in Washington from which we took a cab to the apartment where my buddy's mother resided. My heart was pounding a mile a minute; I found the District of Columbia really impressive. The rowhouses, block after block, and the massive buildings one right after another plus the incredible traffic were eye openers for a boy who had just come from the farm. The president's wife, "Bess" Truman, was to be in the audience at our concert, but for one reason or another, she didn't make it. Still the concert was a great success. We sang the next day at Washington's Children's Hospital. After lunch, we went out to Mt. Vernon. It was at the tomb of George Washington that we sang the anthems, "This is My Country" and "The Battle Hymn of the Republic."

After the first of the year, members of the senior class began preparing for two very special occasions: a formal Valentine's Day dance and, of course, the senior prom. We had already been fitted for and received our "class rings," and our senior pictures had been taken, so lots of activity was filling our calendars; the year was passing quickly. Our "formal" dances were held in the social room of the community building; it was a lovely setting for an event of this kind. Formal, for us, meant that we should buy our date a corsage and that she would be in an evening gown. Each of the boys was attired in his Sunday suit.

During the winter of '46-'47, the Band began its preparation for the big on-stage concert, held each spring in the big theatre of the community building.

The Memorial Day parade was also on the band's schedule, and that would be the last time that I would march as drum major of the H.I.S. Band.

The Glee Club prepared for its annual spring concert. This was held in the auditorium on "The Hill," but it was preceded with forensic competition at Johnstown, PA., where the Glee Club won the state championship! The Octet placed but did not win first place.

In early summer, we took final exams, knowing that it was all over except for the shouting and celebrating. Seniors, at this point, were looked upon as "having arrived." The junior class was skipping into each new day, knowing that very, very soon, they would be at the top.

Honors Day was held in conjunction with graduation weekend. We were gathered in the auditorium on "The Hill." Academically, I was not a stand out, so I just sat back and enjoyed watching my classmates receive their awards. I was absolutely stunned to hear my name called and at that moment to learn that I was to receive a monetary award for excellent service as drum major of the Band! It was an exhilarating and unforgettable moment for me.

The events of graduation weekend were inspiring. Sunday morning, the senior class filed into chapel with the eyes of the student body on us. It was an emotional experience; we knew that this would be the last time, as students, we would share together in worship. That hour would never, could never, be relived. After Monday evening, we would be graduates; it would never be the same again. The next chapel service that we would attend would be as members of the alumni association. So it was with solemnity and, frankly, with a few tears that we were last to file in and the first to leave chapel that day.

Now we were on stage, in our assigned seats, ready for the commencement exercise to begin. We weren't processing and neither were we in cap and gown. Our garb was a brand new suit, a new shirt and tie, and new shoes on our feet. On our coat lapel was pinned a rose — not just any rose, we were wearing an M. S. Hershey rose, beautiful because of its specialty. Mr. Hershey would have been proud of every one of us — his boys!

Eleven years earlier he opened his arms to me, an orphan. As I sat on stage that evening of graduation, there were three things that I wished:

1. that I had been a more dedicated student,

2. that my grandparents could have been there to share in the joy of the occasion, and

3. that Mr. Hershey could have been with us to personally hand us our diplomas.

In my musings, I realized that my younger brother Albert, my buddies who were a year or two behind me, and the other Homeboys out there in the audience were going to be sorely missed. This was my home; they were my family. My one sister, Minerva, who had recently married, had come from Pittsburgh to be there for my graduation. She had ridden the Greyhound bus which had been my source of transportation on those occasions when I went for the annual two-week summer vacation. She arrived in early afternoon the day of commencement, and some friends of mine took her to the bus station in Harrisburg for her return trip that very evening. She was the only Hobby on hand for my "big day." While I didn't realize it then, I now know that it was a sacrifice for her to make the trip.

We were informed that the curtain was about to open. When it did, we were on stage looking at a full house. The community building's big theatre was the setting for the commencement exercise. It was truly exciting. Each of us had his name called, signaling the moment to walk across the stage. At the center ready to greet us were W. Allen Hammond, H.I.S. Principal, and D. Paul Witmer, Superintendent, who presented to us that precious document for which each of us had been working and anticipating.

I heard my name: Clark E. Hobby. Can it be true? Had the time come? In our alma mater, we sang the words: "*...there comes a time when we bid thee goodbye...*" The time had come and now I

The Homeboy's Senior Picture.

wasn't certain that I was ready to leave. Clutching my diploma, I completed the walk, arriving back at my seat. When I thought it safe to do so, I opened it, and there I had proof...I had satisfied all the requirements for graduation.

Soon the exercise was over. The curtain closed. The reality of the situation was setting in. Turning to each other, we graduates realized, "This is it, guys!" Those who were up on stage and were recognized as graduates were brothers with whom we had grown up. Some of us had begun the journey together as far back as the second grade; some even earlier. We hugged and cried as we said goodbye. This event that was concluding was more than a celebration of graduation from high school, we were at the end of a home life as well. The next morning, class members would be leaving, and as a class, we knew that we would never, ever be in the same place at the same time again.

Being on stage that evening was thrilling, but it was also a sad occasion for us. That night we knew that no matter how far we would go or how old we would grow, there was one thing that would never change. We shared a precious bond that would never be broken:

WE WERE HOMEBOYS!

X.
EPILOGUE

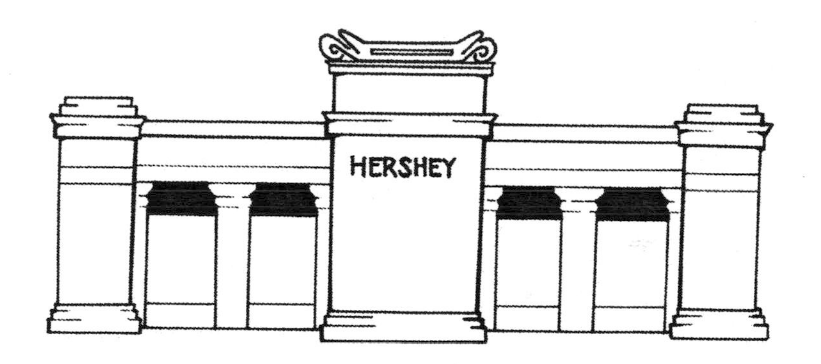

WHAT HAPPENED TO THE HOMEBOY?

After graduation, with three of my classmates, I enlisted in the U.S. Army Air Corps, which during my tenure became the U.S. Air Force. Following basic training, two of the Homeboys, Dick and Jack, were transferred to Wyoming, while "Bo" and I were sent to Lowry Air Base, Denver, Colorado.

When we finished our schooling, "Bo" was sent to Japan, and I transferred to Chanute Air Base located at Rantoul, Illinois, with an assignment of chaplain's assistant. Within one year of my enlistment two things occurred:

- My job description was changed to Welfare Specialist, with an office in the chapel.
- I was promoted to the rank of sergeant.

A friend of mine directed the choir at the Lutheran Church in Rantoul, and one evening he invited me to accompany him to a choir rehearsal. It was there that I met my wife, Betty. We were engaged in March of 1949 and in August of that year we were married. It was while I served with the Air Force that our first child, a daughter, was born. Upon separation from the military, I tried several different jobs. At the time, jobs were not plentiful and the hourly rate of pay was very low. Within nineteen months our second child, a son, was born, and eighteen months after that my wife gave birth to our third child, another daughter. In the meantime, I began working a part-time job to supplement my income. The part-time job was as a salesman in a men's clothing store. I proved to be quite good at selling and was offered a full-time job in the clothing store, assisting the manager. The change brought a salary which enabled me to focus on the one job. However, I was spending a lot of time at the Lutheran Church in Rantoul. I sang in a quartet and with the choir, and I served as the church's organist.

For several years I resisted a call to the ministry, but in time it became crystal clear to me that I would never experience fulfillment until I did what God was calling me to do. One evening, after closing the men's store, I arrived home ready to talk seriously with my wife about God's call. The children were already in bed.

I asked my wife to sit on the couch because I needed to talk with her. After sharing with her what I knew God was calling me to do, I could tell that she was visibly shaken. After all, we had three children, a new home in which we had lived for only two years and an automobile that was just a year old. The hill that we would climb together was steep to say the least. I would need four years of college and four years in seminary to qualify for ordination. With a wife and three children, that seemed a mission impossible.

All night, my wife cried. The next morning she asked, "What do we have to do to get started?" We sold both the car and the house. The University of

Illinois was located thirty miles away, and it was the institution in which I matriculated; in fact, our first child started first grade the very same day that I began attending classes at the university. I was twenty-six years of age. There were many who questioned my ability to survive academically and financially. All the while, my wife and I were learning about the amazing grace and the incredible providence of God.

Sunday after Sunday I listened to a pastor preach sermons that emphasized this truth: "When God calls, He provides!" We went through some extremely difficult times. When we wondered where the next meal would come from, there was a knock at the door and/or a letter in the mail bringing encouraging assistance.

I had the privilege of serving two student churches, prior to my ordination. After graduating from the University of Illinois, I was given a contract to teach in the public school concurrent with divinity school studies. This I did while serving a little parish as a student pastor. Time passed quickly. The year prior to completing my divinity degree, our fourth child, another son, was born.

During the years of my ministry, I served two mission congregations, two large congregations and one of medium size. In each of the pastorates, I had opportunity to lead in building programs, making use of the training that I received at "The Home," studying the carpentry course. The ability to read blueprints and to understand specifications proved to be invaluable.

Working with youth has been a strong part of my ministry. Each year I have taken my church's high school youth on an annual "trip with pastor." The purpose of the trip has been spiritual enrichment blended with seeing new places and meeting new people within the Christian context.

Looking back on my life, it is clear that what I received at "The Home" by way of discipline, a sense of loyalty, a work ethic and the embracing of lofty values enabled me to become a better person, a faithful servant of the Lord, a loving father and grandfather and one who seeks to be responsive to the needs of others.

By God's grace and with His help, I live each new day with a growing appreciation of the eleven years that I spent as a Homeboy. It is gratifying to know that Milton Hershey School goes on in perpetuity offering to needy kids a home and school. All of us who were the recipients of the nurturing of "The Home" need to take seriously the words of Jesus, "To whom much has been given, much is required."

I feel strongly that it was by the providence of God that I was sent to the Hershey Industrial School, now known as the Milton Hershey School.

What I have put on paper is my story; it is a story not unlike thousands of others who were and today are the recipients of the generosity and philanthropy of Milton S. Hershey, the Chocolate King, and his wife, Catherine. The Hershey legacy lives on in perpetuity.

At Mr. Hershey's funeral, The Reverend John H. Treder in closing remarks said:

"To you eight seniors who bear your friend to his resting place, I address these words:

> You represent today, all the boys of the school, a high honor. We regret that all (the boys) could not be with us. When you go back to your mates, please tell them this, and ask them to join you and all of us in this community, the Directors of this school, and those of the township schools of the Corporation, of the Estates, of the Banks, all of us of whatever rank or file, the young and the old - in the pledge we make this day to our founding father, that as we enter this new era in the life of our community, we shall go forward in the spirit in which it was founded and with the same vision.
>
> That we may be strengthened in this resolve we raise to God...those ancient words men were taught to pray in that far-off promised land:
>
> > 'Look down, O God from Thy holy habitation from Heaven and bless us Thy People, and the land,

this community, which Thou hast given us, a land that truly floweth with milk and honey.'

And now, Mr. Hershey, we commend you to the tender mercies of God, praying that He will receive you, freed from sin, more and more into His presence; that perchance you may hear in Paradise His voice,

'Inasmuch as ye have done it unto one of the least of these my brethren, ye have done it unto me.'" *

I was one of the least, and all thanks and praise be to God, I was given the blessing of being one of "Milton's boys." *Yes, I was...and I will always be a Homeboy!*

* The School Industrialist, November, 1945, p. 24.

MILTON HERSHEY SCHOOL
1999

Today, Mr. Hershey's endowment continues to provide nurturing and education for approximately 1,300 boys and girls in grades kindergarten through grade twelve. At the School, children receive a well-rounded education enhanced by the latest technology.

Students live in the safe, supportive, family-like environment of student homes under the guidance of houseparents-married couples with specialized training in child care and child development who care for 8-12 students in each home. A certification program developed by MHS provides additional professional child care education for all houseparents.

The MHS-designed Parenting Model supports houseparents in their role as surrogate parents and provides guiding principles and practices about topics such as family, human worth, responsibility, individuality, hope professionalism and quality of life.

School focus is on personal attention to each student's needs. The School has developed a set of "Desired Results" to prepare each student for work and further study. They are designed to help each child grow and mature into an educated, responsible, productive, self-motivated adult, as well as ensure each student learns and practices good citizenship.

INFORMATION ABOUT ADMISSIONS IS AVAILABLE FROM THE OFFICE OF ADMISSIONS, (717)520-2100 OR TOLL FREE 1-800-322-3248. THE SCHOOL ALSO HAS AN INTERNET HOMEPAGE: www.hershey.pvt.k12.pa.us.